A Debt to the Dead

A Debt to the Dead

Michael Kellichner

Elsewhen Press

A Debt to the Dead
First published in Great Britain by Elsewhen Press, 2025
An imprint of Alnpete Limited

Copyright © Michael Kellichner, 2025. All rights reserved
The right of Michael Kellichner to be identified as the author of this work has been asserted in accordance with sections 77 and 78 of the Copyright, Designs and Patents Act 1988. No part of this publication may be reproduced, scanned, stored in a retrieval system or transmitted in any form, or by any means (electronic, mechanical, telepathic, magical, or otherwise) without the prior written permission of the copyright owner. No part of this book may be used or reproduced in any manner for the purpose of training artificial intelligence technologies or systems. In accordance with Article 4(3) of the Digital Single Market Directive 2019/790, Elsewhen Press expressly reserves this work from the text and data mining exception.

Elsewhen Press, PO Box 757, Dartford, Kent DA2 7TQ
www.elsewhen.press

British Library Cataloguing in Publication Data.
A catalogue record for this book is available from the British Library.

ISBN 978-1-915304-84-1 Print edition
ISBN 978-1-915304-94-0 eBook edition

Condition of Sale
This book is sold subject to the condition that it shall not, by way of trade or otherwise, be lent, re-sold, hired out or otherwise circulated in any form of binding or cover other than that in which it is published and without a similar condition including this condition being imposed on the subsequent purchaser.

This book is copyright under the Berne Convention.
Elsewhen Press & Planet-Clock Design are trademarks of Alnpete Limited

Designed and formatted by Elsewhen Press

As part of our environmental awareness approach, in a bid to reduce paper and ink usage, the print edition of this book has minimal margins and leading, and the body of the text is typeset in Adobe Garamond Pro that typically requires 27% less ink than Times New Roman. We use Print on Demand to reduce wastage and unnecessary transportation and storage.

This book is a work of fiction. All names, characters, places, and events are either a product of the author's fertile imagination or are used fictitiously. Any resemblance to actual events, places or people (living or dead – human, elf, dwarf, or god) is purely coincidental.

Contents

Chapter 1: The Legend

Anuhea was sitting on the floor, drunk, in darkness, when a fluttering through the room roused him from his half-slumber. He pushed back the knotted tangles of black hair falling across his sharp features and slid his hand around until he found the earthen jug full of sour spirits. He took another drink and blinked thickly. His eyes settled on the open window where frigid winter air whistled in with faint ghosts of snow. He couldn't remember leaving it open. He felt hot and sweaty despite the cold, and pushed away some of the destitute rags and moldy blankets he'd piled about himself.

A nightingale flitted down and landed on the toe of his boot. Anuhea squinted for a moment, then turned his foot, expecting the bird to take flight again. But it remained motionless and stared at him with one beady eye. Anuhea shrugged and started to lift the jug again.

"Are you Anuhea the Many-Handed?" the nightingale asked.

After a pause, Anuhea murmured, "Now this is a first." His voice was thick and hoarse, both from the drink and from atrophy. He sat up a little straighter and cleared his throat. "A talking bird? And one that speaks perfect Elvish?" He let the jug thunk against the floorboards and contemplated it. "I must have swiped a bad batch."

The bird sat preternaturally motionless on his boot, its head turned so one depthless black eye trained on his face. The gaze was piercing, and it made Anuhea shift under its scrutiny. The bird didn't flutter as his boot moved across the floor; only its head adjusted to continue staring at him.

"Could it be that a legend is in such a state, so deep in his cups?" the bird asked.

Anuhea looked to each side and smirked. "I'm not sure where you're looking," he said, "but there aren't any cups to be found here." He lifted the jug, tilted it toward the nightingale for emphasis, and tipped it back. The last few drops trickled out, and Anuhea wiped his mouth with his sleeve. He set the jug down, rolled it away, and started to stand with a groan. The nightingale fluttered off his boot and perched on the windowsill, a black shadow against blacker sky.

Anuhea wavered, watching the bird. He looked about the small room, an old, abandoned woodcutter's cabin with a leaking roof and drafty walls. Outside a wet wind howled, creaking the ancient timber and making the door shudder in its frame. The wind whistled through the imperfect boards and finally Anuhea shivered. He dug through his rag pile until he found his cloak, dusty and frayed but still thick enough to bring some warmth back to his shoulders.

He tripped over some of the blankets, stumbled, managed to stay upright, and went to the shelf above a small stove. "Well, whatever it was that loosed your tongue," he said, looking up at three more jugs, "one of these will put it back in order." Even with his back turned, he could feel the bird's scrutinizing eye taking in every movement as he blew into his hands, rubbed them together, and brought another jug down. He bit the cork and pulled it out. The feeling of the gaze at his back, though, made him waver and just stand there holding the jug.

"This world has changed so much," the nightingale said. "But I had not realized it had changed enough to leave a legend so disgraced."

Anuhea pressed a palm against the side of his head. "There's that word again. 'Legend.' Such a heavy word. Too heavy. Can't carry something so heavy around. It'll tire you out." He stretched his jaw. "An old word. An old word in an older tongue." He turned. "I thought birds were supposed to sing?"

"Will you not answer me plainly?"

"That cadence. That inflection." His eyes narrowed and he looked down at the jug in his hand as if it had answers to questions he couldn't quite formulate. "You're part of the old world for certain. One of the royal court, perhaps? Though I don't recall any birds fluttering around the throne." He shrugged and smirked again. "Though perhaps," he said, lifting the jug, "strange things happened at night in the castle."

He drank, and, fortified, looked at the sill where the bird slowly collected a dusting of snow. "Come closer, then. Let me see this bird that speaks with such formality and regalness."

The nightingale fluttered to the floor and stood there, looking up at Anuhea. It remained there with a statuesque solidity unnatural in a bird.

"A ghost, perhaps?" Anuhea crouched down and rested his forearms languidly on his knees. His body was bony, all sharp angles. The jug hung limply in his fingers. The wind outside whistled through the walls and the hut's creaking grew so loud for a moment it made the room feel like it was tilting, about to tumble down the mountain. "Of all the ghosts I seek, why does some bird arrive? So what was it? Did I shoot a sure arrow to pluck you from the sky to win a bet? Am I to be haunted for such a senseless act, now?" He looked up at the window, out into the night and where he knew behind thick clouds the sky was filled with stars all in the wrong places. "When will the haunts for my greater sins arrive, then?"

"I am neither spirit nor ghost," the nightingale said. "I come seeking the aid of Anuhea the Many-Handed, as he was known in the human lands."

"Well, Anuhea you have found." His tone slipped lower and into a cadence mocking the formal rhythm of the old elvish aristocracy with which the bird spoke. He set the jug down and splayed his fingers. "But, alas, he who has only two hands. Not many."

"Are there many Anuheas in the world that I have mistaken you for another?"

Anuhea smirked. "When the world ended, everyone in it changed. Perhaps there are other Anuheas, now. Perhaps I am no longer the one you seek."

He stood and drank. "But fear not, small creature. I still remember kindness that was taught to me, and I will not turn you out into the cold." He went to the cupboards and began opening the doors at random. "I believe I have some ill-gotten bread that we can break."

"Are you the Anuhea who stood against the new god while the world was sundering?"

The bird didn't move as Anuhea's entire body tightened and he spun around to face it. He took a step sideways, as if seeing the bird from another angle would shatter an illusion shrouding its true form. "Ghost?" He sneered. "My mistake. Begone, demon, and leave me to whatever small peace this world has left for me."

His hand shook and sloshed spirits from the jug. He lifted it, lowered it, went to gesture with it, and finally spun toward the door. "Are there more of you, then? Did he send you?" He ripped off his cloak and clomped to the door. "If he did, he'd better have sent more than one bird." He threw open the door. A gale rushed in, blowing in the snow that had already accumulated on the ground. It spiraled across the floorboards and, outside, the creaking of all the leafless trees farther down from where the cabin was tucked against a sheer wall of stone. Wind whipped his hair, howled like a beast.

There was nothing except snow, darkness, and wind. Anuhea looked up, searching the sky for the burning red star that housed the god he had attempted to defeat, but thick clouds obscured the sky. Even then, Anuhea scoured for even the tiniest split in the cover that would allow that god to peek through and see him.

A flutter near his ear and the tiny, phantasmal weight of the nightingale touched against his shoulder. Anuhea whirled, and the bird alighted. He swung the jug, narrowly missed it, and followed it back into the room. The wind whipped the door shut with a crack that shook the cabin. The bird landed on the windowsill again, but had to fly when Anuhea threw the jug. It smashed against the wall, exploding jagged chunks of hardened clay and a spray of spirits. The nightingale swooped down, and banked to go to the shelves, but Anuhea's hand snatched out and plucked the bird from the air.

Anuhea lifted his hand so the bird was level with his eyes. "Whoever told you about me must not have known me very well. If you thought a few years and being a drunk would make me sluggish enough to not catch a bird, you were mistaken." He tightened his grip, but the nightingale still didn't struggle or look away. "I am the Anuhea you seek, yes, bird. One foolish enough to try and stab a god through the heart, and one that is foolish enough to try again if he were here. And what are you? Some sad, sorry betrayer of our race? Some follower of this new god, chasing down all who have ever opposed him?"

"There is no love in me for the new god nor his followers," the nightingale said. "I come on behalf of House Nightbreeze."

At the name, Anuhea flicked the bird away as if it were a hot coal. It fluttered back to the windowsill and sat like a statue watching him. Anuhea's hand remained outstretched and trembling for a few seconds before finally dropping limply to his side. The rest of his body sagged, as if the weight of his hand was suddenly so great it would pull him down to the floor.

"Nightbreeze," he murmured. "If you're not a spirit or a ghost, there is nothing remaining from that house that means anything to me. Once, yes. But not for a long time." He looked down at his hands, tried to curl his fingers, but they stopped as hooks, trembling, and unable to close. He stared at them and tried to will them shut, but the trembling only traveled up his arm, and finally he seized his elbows and hugged his arms against his stomach to try and stop the shaking. "Though perhaps you are more than you appear and I do not give you enough credit. You are a talking bird, after all. Perhaps you can cross to the realms of the dead and return?"

A flash of memory—endless sky, tumbling rocks, and a roar

louder than a hundred dragons—sent him reaching for another jug, but his fingers only curled around the shelf's edge. He tried to open them, but they were locked onto the wood, his arms trembling. "And even if you could, what could you tell me that I don't already know? That I can't already imagine? That I want to stop imagining, no matter what." He pried his fingers off the shelf and turned. A small smirk formed as he said, "And though I've been drinking away my memories, I'm confident that there were no birds perched in the Nightbreeze family tree."

"I am Astra of the Wilds. I come on behalf of Ivellios Nightbreeze, the sole surviving member of the house."

For a moment the name meant nothing to Anuhea, and it rattled around inside his head like a stone in an empty cup. He could only remember Tinnu, and that was the reason he was trying to forget everything. To remember anyone else, he'd have to remember what she said, risk remembering her voice. Even brushing close enough to such a thought made his head throb and the shaking in his hands worsen. He stretched for a jug, but only managed to knock one off the shelf. It shattered on the floor as he managed to grab the other. He pulled it down and bit into the cork to pull it out, but bit too viciously and his teeth went straight through.

His shaking fingers tried to grip the tiny remainder of cork, but as he repeatedly failed, his memory was filled with too much light. The roar returned, and he clenched the jar so tightly his arms quivered. He grit his teeth against the image of trees tearing from the soil, roots and bedrock all tumbling into fissures ripping through the earth. The world sundering. But somewhere from the other side of that memory he remembered hearing the name Ivellios before.

"Her brother," he muttered. He spit out the ruined cork. "So he managed to survive the apocalypse?" He pressed a finger against the remaining cork, trying to shove it into the jug.

"We survived, yes. Though barely."

"Better than most." The cork didn't budge. "Even so, I never met him. I don't owe him anything, so I'm not sure why he would send you here."

"Much has changed in the time you've been gone, Anuhea," Astra said.

"I don't care anything for this world. There's nothing left in it worth caring about. Let it change."

"The new god is the new power in this world. His rule expands every day, and those loyal to him hunt down any who would oppose him. Any remnants of the old world are to be destroyed. Ivellios and our allies have been fighting him at every turn, but it is trying to hold back a flood."

"I never was a soldier," Anuhea said. He looked around the room for something to get at the cork with. "You've definitely come to the wrong place."

"Even among the youngest in our resistance, your reputation still exists. That in thousands of years of elvish history, you were the only one to escape from the sky prisons, and that you're the only one declared a traitor to not be branded with the traitor's mark."

Anuhea rubbed the spot below his left eye where the brand would have been. Those memories, so long before Tinnu, were enough that the shaking in his hands returned to a faint tremble. "That was a long time ago. But what of it? Do not think that just because you come representing the elvish aristocracy that you have any sway over me. What is your plan? That if I don't help you, you'll drag me back to the sky prisons?"

"All of our allies were killed." The nightingale lowered its head for a moment, but continued. "We were lured into a trap and everyone was killed, except for Ivellios. The order following the new god has captured him and he's being held in their citadel, in the heart of the new empire."

"I understand the new god holds a particular hatred for elves," Anuhea said softly. "Given that more than one tried to stop his ascension." He set the bottle on the stove. "Ivellios is dead. From the little I saw, they have no time for prisoners. Everyone who opposes them get destroyed."

"Ivellios is one of the last who holds many of the old world's secrets. The only surviving member of the queen's personal guard, and talented enough to evade capture and defeat for fifty years. As far as we know, we have been the only group to stand against them for so long. The new order believes he possesses knowledge of the old elvish magic, how to harness it and bend it to the order's will. They are keeping him, torturing him, trying to pry the secrets from him."

"How can you know all this?"

"The rain carries me news from far off. The trees still whisper the rumors floating on wind."

"Will he talk?"

"Never."

Anuhea rubbed his jaw. "The rest of his life is going to be short and miserable."

"We can save him," Astra said.

"Can we now?" Anuhea muttered. He started to lift the jug.

"Are you *not* the legendary thief Anuhea? Rumored to have nearly stolen the queen's jewel's from the room that none other than royalty has even glanced at? If you cannot save someone from that citadel, then there is no one who can manage it left in the world."

"You have come all this way chasing a legend." The bitter twist that had settled on Anuhea's lips unwound. His face softened and he shook his head. He gestured around the cabin, to the liquor jugs, to the broken shards on the floor. To the walls oozing whistling wind. "Sad, sorry hope you had." He looked down at the jug, shook his head, and went to the door. He leaned his head against it, listening to the wind howling past. "And even if I could help you, why would I? It won't change the world. It will just put one more living ghost back in it to wander around."

Astra was silent for a long while. Finally, she said, "I didn't come because of the legends humans and elves tell about you. I came because of a different story I was told about you."

"Lots of people told stories about me," Anuhea said. He looked down at his hand, watching how his fingers trembled. "Which one did you hear? How I stole the moon during an eclipse, but found that it was too easy, so I put it back, hence there is still a moon? How I emptied a noble's hall of everything of value, right down to his silver cutlery, all while he was having his dinner?" He exhaled a short breath, something between a laugh and a scoff. He dropped his hands and looked back at Astra. "Or was it the one about how I once stole a beard off a dwarf? They loved that one. Everyone would always laugh when they heard it." He turned about as if he were trying to find another place to be, as if there were more to find in the single, drafty room.

"I heard that you once found a child lost in the snow," Astra said. At the words, Anuhea snapped around to stare at her dark shadow on the windowsill. "You found her and took her in and put her next to a fire. And when she was warm and fed, you learned she had nowhere to go. So you took her under your wing and taught her everything you knew."

The world was blurry. "Not everything," Anuhea muttered. He wiped his cheeks with the back of his hand. "Who would tell you such a ridiculous story? It doesn't have the ring of legend at all."

"Anuhea," Astra said, "I do not know much about you. But I know enough that had I come to ask your assistance on behalf of the elves, you would turn me away. If I asked you for help out of the goodness in your heart, you would turn me away. That is how you were described in the elf kingdoms. One who possessed no love for our history and culture. You were the great thief and escapist. A traitor. But the one who knew you best told me a very different story in the short time I met her. She spoke of an elf full of kindness even if he couldn't see it himself. Of an elf full of knowledge and skill and the patience to pass it on. If you will not help the last member of Tinnu's house—"

"Don't say her name."

"—then Sadoc has won, we are defeated, and there is no one left in this world who can help me."

Just hearing her name brought the roar of a breaking world back to him. The endless sky. Everything tumbling down except for Sadoc, the new god, rising up. The realization that, for the second time in his entire life, he had failed. He had judged incorrectly and had met an enemy impossible to defeat.

His fingers seized again, and as he tried to pry them apart, he remembered seeing Tinnu after the long time they had been separated. He remembered her telling of her journeys far north to the elf lands—his old homeland that he had not seen in enough years to lose count—to regain the memories that had been stolen from her, that had left so much of her life before they'd met in nothing but a blackness like the bottom of the ocean. How she had found her past there, and how she had found her brother whom she had not even known she had, who had sent her away to save her. She spoke of him with so much love and kindness, in the way only one who has lost someone for so long and then found them again can speak. There had been so much joy when she spoke of him, even though the time between their parting and reunion had been so long that both siblings had changed into nearly unrecognizable versions of themselves.

He realized, again, how much Tinnu had lost. How little remained that would allow her to believe in goodness, yet somehow goodness had been the only thing that had ever guided her. To hear the story of her life was to believe she deserved to hate the world and despise its inhabitants, but she had come out wishing only to help others. After teaching her, he thought that he had understood her deeply, but he had never understood where that goodness came from. How she seemed to possess it without end. Even as he fled from the realities of the world, abandoning her for years, she still possessed love and kindness in her heart when she saw him again.

And all that remained in his world that she had cared about was himself. And Ivellios.

In his memory, the world was filled with too much light.

He pressed his shaking palm against his temple. "You said Ivellios is being held captive?"

"Yes."

"And you're certain he is alive?" He pressed harder. "That they would not have already killed him?"

"Yes."

He brought up the other palm, as if he were trying to keep his head from splitting apart. Both hands shook, but he managed to push down the memory of the shattering world. "In a citadel. How many people would be in this citadel?"

"Hundreds."

Old gears in his head tried to start turning, the part of him that parsed every piece of information before accepting a job, before planning a heist. Every detail organized, scrutinized in order to begin to formulate a plan, and that plan tested to ensure that nothing could go wrong. Endless possibilities, whittled down with further questions, more information. But all he could imagine was a foreboding castle against a blinding sky and legions of soldiers in his way.

"All loyal to the new god, I presume?" he said, lowering to the ground, his knees against his chest.

"The most loyal he has in the entire empire."

Anuhea's body stilled, and his hands stopped quivering. He lifted his head and rested his arms across his knees, and looked at the dark spot of the nightingale on the windowsill. Old words tried to form on his tongue—words from before, when life was lighter and the world lacked seriousness. When everything was still a game, and he was faster than anyone who would try to catch him. "I knew she would cause me no end of trouble," was one remark, but he couldn't bring himself to say it, even in jest. "Only hundreds? Glad they made it easy for me," was another, but he had seen the viciousness of those loyal to the new god, and what they did to any who opposed them. The flicker of their memory made his shoulders sag, remembering how easy the world used to be and how heavily it weighed on him now.

He couldn't bring himself to remember Tinnu, even though he knew she would have already been out the door and halfway down the mountain as soon as she learned that her brother had been captured. She would get the details on the journey, without a thought whether it would be possible. While he struggled to not remember her face, to not remember how her jaw tensed when she was focused on a problem, the faces of his other old companions, those who had been with him when he had found Tinnu in the streets, alone in the snow, returned to his memory. He saw their stern faces, and, for the first time in years, they were not coated with the cold pallor of death. Their mouths did not fall open and black, bloated tongues did not fall from their mouths. They did not stare at him with white, glassy eyes. He remembered them as they had been in the tavern, warmed by the fire on a winter night, cheeks rosy with ale. All looking at him with stern expectation, the look they had when he had first thought to turn Tinnu back out into the street.

"None of them will ever forgive me," he said and shook his head. "I wouldn't ever be able to die. I'd have to listen to them scold me for all eternity."

Astra cocked her head to the side.

"I want you to know something. I'm not doing this to help you. I don't know Ivellios. I've never met him, I don't owe him anything. I don't owe the elves a thing. I don't owe this world anything. I couldn't care less about any of you. There's nothing any living elf possesses that would make me help them." He stood, staggered, and leaned heavily against the wall.

"But Ivellios is all that's left of her in this world." He couldn't speak for a few minutes after saying it. His chest tightened and he struggled to breathe. "And she would want me to save him. If I don't save him, if the chance ever comes, how could I ever face her again? I owe her that. I owe her at least this much."

He drew a shaking breath. "You have my word, Astra of the Wilds. I'll get Ivellios out of the citadel. I swear on my debt to the dead, and I won't go and see them again without fulfilling it."

His hand was shaking again. He pushed hair out of his face and spit the lingering taste of cheap liquor out of his mouth. "So where are we going?"

Chapter 2: The Obstacles

Anuhea pulled the window shut and stacked fresh wood into the stove. Crouched there, trying to get a spark from his flint and steel to catch on the kindling, he was aware of the bottle on the shelf high above him. He ignored it, finally got a small ember to glow, and gently breathed until it was flickering with faint life. Even the tiny heat made his skin prickle, like ice was thawing in his pores, but he kept his face close, breathing steadily into the base of the growing flame.

"The world has changed much since you abandoned it," Astra said from her perch on the windowsill.

"I was there," Anuhea said. He fed in a few twigs and watched as the flame spread. "I saw Sadoc rip it apart."

"And now it has been put back together. His followers have rebuilt. They have a new capital city in the heart of a fledgling empire. A city already so sprawling that it rivals the largest human cities of the old world."

"Good," Anuhea said. He added some bark pieces and placed his hands in front of the meager fire, soaking up some warmth. The heat helped his fingers relax and he could almost feel them fully again. He breathed into the fire once more to help it spread. "The more people in one place, the easier it is to go about and not be noticed. So where is it?"

"It is in the center of the second continent."

He looked back over his shoulder. "The second continent?"

"When Sadoc ripped apart the world, he did not put it back together in the way of old. He has left four great continents floating in endless sky. The second continent is home to all his followers, the humans who have flocked to him in the aftermath of the world ending. They have spread across the land, driving out the other races who have attempted to survive and claiming everything they touch in the name of the new god."

Anuhea nodded. "How far is it from here?" His hands warmed, he rubbed his face, steeled himself, and shoved aside the pile of rags, cloaks, and blankets he'd been nested in when Astra arrived. He worked a finger into a tiny space between two floorboards and lifted one up.

"We will need to cross the endless sky to reach him. Several days of travel."

Anuhea pulled up another board and paused to blow into his

hands, bringing a tiny bit more warmth to his fingers. "Sounds far," he said. He looked back at her. "Too far. How did you know I was here?"

Astra cocked her head to the side. "It hardly seems pertinent at the moment."

"I fled to the farthest place from civilization I could find," Anuhea said. "Since the world's end, no one has come up this mountain except me. Until you fly in through my window. How could you ever find me up here?"

Astra emitted a low, whistling trill that could only be a sigh. "As you fled, you passed many ancient and wise trees. Even as years pass by, trees retain their knowledge and those who survived the sundering of the world recalled your passage. More recently, a ferret, a mouse, a squirrel noted the passing of an elf in lands that had not been trodden by anything other than an animal in years."

"So many eyes to worry about that I never would have concerned myself with." He smirked. "I suppose I should be thankful I've never counted a Wild One as one of my enemies." He pulled up two more boards and sat back, looking into the dark hole beneath the floor. "So how will we reach the second layer, then? Your kind always kept to themselves, so little was known about you and your strange magic, but I presume you will take the form of a larger winged beast and I shall ride upon your back? Tales at least told how Wild Ones change their skin like others change their clothes."

"You, who possess so many tales about yourself, would believe such rumors about the Wild Ones?"

Anuhea shook his head and smirked. "I suppose what others say about you isn't always true. However, you are here, an elf in a bird's body, so I suspect at least some of the rumor is true."

Astra was silent for a moment before saying, "Were we in time before, yes, this would be an option. However I have lost nearly all of my power, and this form is the only one I am capable of maintaining for any length of time."

Anuhea chewed his cheek as he thought, but didn't turn back to her. "You've become so weak that you cannot even become an elf again? I don't know much about Wild Ones and their abilities, but have the rules of magic changed that much since Sadoc's ascension that you cannot draw power from your homeland anymore?"

"Much has changed, yes," Astra said. "However, there is another way."

"Hidden magic roads?" Anuhea said. He reached down into the

hole and pulled up a cracked, dusty, weathered leather satchel. "An old friend knew something or two about them. Couldn't ever find one, but seems scholars all agreed there were roads forged by ancient magic traversing the world. Wizards used them, but then they just up and lost where they were."

"If they existed, they surely have shattered with the world," Astra said.

Anuhea shifted to directly in front of the fire. The soft light washed over the old leather and as he wiped away the thick film of dust, his hands started to tremble. The leather was plain and limp from years of use. Just brushing against the surface was enough to threaten to fill his head with memories.

"Sadoc's empire has utilized magic to create fleets of airships that it uses to move between the four layers," Astra said. "It is how his armies march to the farthest reaches of the empire quickly and how he brings stone and metal to a land he has arranged without mountains. Ivellios and I managed to steal one from his followers, and we have been using it to escape and strike deeper and deeper into the heart of their territory."

"Fortuitous," Anhea said. His fingers shook and he struggled with the knot on the satchel's strings. "So we hop on this airship and fly to the second layer."

"At the moment we cannot," Astra said. "The core of the ship requires a constant supply of magical energy to keep the ship in the air. We counted a wizard in our resistance, and she allowed us to move quickly and efficiently. But she was killed along with the rest when Ivellios was captured."

"I assume you only survived because you were a bird at the time." Anuhea let out a long exhale. He flexed his fingers, stretched them, but they continued to tremble. "Alright, so we have an airship that can't fly, but it's the only way to the second layer. Then first we find a wizard."

"Also impossible. The church hunts down anyone with magical abilities. If they do not willingly join the empire's ranks, they are captured and killed at best. At worst, they are chained in one of the airships while the ship feeds off their magic and they remain there until they die. There have been no wizards operating in the open outside of those loyal to the empire in ten years."

"So we have a ship that cannot fly and there are no more wizards who could fly it." Anuhea managed to work out the knot and opened the satchel. Inside was a leather bundle that he withdrew.

"Certainly there are some wizards still working in secret, but we do not have the luxury of time in finding them out. Especially in this part of the world, the task might indeed be impossible."

"I presume your magic doesn't work?"

"Flying over endless sky where there are no trees, no animals, nothing to draw upon the magic of the land would have us plummeting within minutes if we relied on my power. However, there is still one great source in this world that Sadoc does not know about. I believe we can use it to power the airship. Possibly forever."

"Some old artifact," Anuhea mumbled. He turned the bundle about in his hands. "Good to know."

He unrolled the leather bundle and his tools appeared, exactly as he had laid them out when he'd packed them away. His set of steel lock picks, metal files, a small hammer, tiny chisels, a flint and steel, his whittling knife, his boot knife. Then, on either end, still flawless in their leather sheaths, his elvish daggers, hilts glowing faintly green in the lamplight.

"So where is this artifact?" he asked.

"In the heart of the elvish lands."

Anuhea turned. "The elf lands?"

It had been nearly a hundred years since he had left the forests behind for the human kingdoms, escaping in the night with only a few supplies and the queen's guard chasing him, the border guards hunting him. He had stolen one of their boats and rowed across the massive river separating the two lands in the middle of the night. The air had been clear, and ahead had been great plains of rolling hills. The eye had so much more distance to see and above him instead of the thick canopy of leaves was an unending sprawl of stars. He had flopped back in the boat, simply staring, feeling the wind and listening to the water, and realized that this was what he had been chasing his entire life. Freedom.

He had never looked back, but he had also never forgotten his time there, what he had learned, and what he had willingly given up for the freedom of the road. He had never possessed a thought or desire to return, and when he had occasionally caught news coming from the forests, it seemed that the nobility was happy enough for him to stay away.

He cleared his throat. "You already know that I was to be exiled, but escaped before they could brand me. I don't think I need to remind you that I'm not exactly welcome there anymore." He drew one of the daggers and held it up for her to see the insignia of the queen's guard inscribed on the blade. "Do you think someone who has stolen two of these can just walk back into elf lands?"

At the sight of the daggers, Astra remained stationary and silent. After a moment, she said, "You will find our homeland quite changed."

"So you keep saying about things. Have they really changed so much that they won't recognize me on sight and throw me back into the sky prisons?"

"Yes."

A heavy chain gripped his chest. There was a seriousness with the way Astra spoke, what details she included and what she did not. Usually, Anuhea could easily tell by someone's face how much they were hiding, but the bird's unchanging expression robbed him of an old crutch, and it deepened his dread. To imagine his homeland so changed meant that something terrible had happened. The elf lands were slow to adapt, slower to change—the race was old and stuck in its ways, and that was part of what had driven Anuhea from them into the world of humans. But it had always lingered in the back of his mind, a solidity that he knew would always exist in the world, even if he was never going to return.

He rolled up his tools again and returned them to the satchel. "As you keep saying," Anuhea said, "this world has changed. I do not know the way back home anymore." Even the words felt awkward in his mouth, as if they were never meant for him to speak.

"This layer is one of rich resources," Astra said. "Sadoc has placed the mountains of the world across this layer, but has also placed our homeland to the north. The northern mountains of our homeland are now the southern border between the land of mountains and the forest. It is not as long a journey as you might have otherwise made."

"Maybe there's something in my heart still wanting home," Anuhea said, and gave a humorless laugh. "Hiding away closer than I ever went when I was running from it? Maybe just more of life's odd ironies."

He looped the satchel over his shoulder, put his cloak back on, and gave one last look at the final bottle of spirits sitting in the shadow. He reached up, grabbed it, and shoved it into his satchel. "I suppose its time," he said, though it seemed like he was talking to the walls and dust instead of Astra. To the spirits lingering in the darkness. "Time to go back into the world again."

He turned abruptly and went out into the night, kicking the door open and letting the wind slam it shut behind him. A second later, Astra landed on his shoulder, burrowed herself in the fur of his hood. The wind whisked away the little heat he'd absorbed from the fire, and it wasn't long before his fingers and toes were numb again.

The cabin was situated just above the tree line against an outcropping of rock where the strongest wind wouldn't hit it. In every direction, more and more peaks dotted the landscape, the space between dipping into valleys full of skeletal trees and snow. Above, thick layers of black clouds obscured the sky full of stars in the wrong places, the empty spots where old stars had been. A new, meaningless sky that made the world seem like it was directionless and every road led nowhere. The wind howled and created ghosts from the snow.

"Storms and a broken sky," Anuhea muttered. "Can't ever tell which way is which anymore."

"North is into the wind," Astra said. "Toward the brewing storm."

He rubbed his eyes, blew into his hands, and pulled his cloak more tightly around himself. Despite the darkness, Anuhea's keen eyes could still make out the mountains and the paths. He scanned his options for a few minutes before deciding to follow one of the higher ridges that kept him above the treeline, exposed to the wind, but would send him to the next peak with half the effort. His brain was still sluggish, as were his limbs, though more and more feeling was returning as he began to sober, but all it led to was needling stabs of cold.

The going was slow and he struggled with his balance. The snow had thawed and frozen repeatedly, been rearranged by the wind, and he kept slipping on unseen ice patches. Each skid and slip almost sent him down, and several times he needed to scramble to avoid sliding down a steep embankment and into the tree line far below. But also the world kept tilting and spinning and losing focus, and the taste of spirits kept rising into the back of his throat. His stomach was a churning, burning ball that kept threatening to escape out his mouth.

He had more questions, but shouting over the wind took too much energy and he focused on dragging his feet through the shin-deep snow. He was halfway to the next peak when fresh flakes began to fall. The wind worsened, slinging sprays of icy crust from the ground against his face. By the time he reached the next peak, the fur lining of his hood was frozen.

"Any chance you could magic this storm away for a bit?" Anuhea said through gritted teeth. "Didn't Wild Ones control the weather?"

"Nothing in nature is controlled," Astra said. "That was not our job. We requested. We asked. Using nature to gain your own whims always ends in destruction."

Anuhea knelt down to catch his breath and try to get less wind blowing over him. "Fine, then," he said. "Can you kindly ask the storm to stop?"

"This is no ordinary storm," Astra said. "It is the agony of the world from its sundering. It is the world's anger manifest, and even if I did commune with the storm, there is too much fury here for it to be reasoned with."

Anuhea shook his head, squeezed his eyes shut against the world going out of focus, continued on with gritted teeth. It wasn't long before his legs ached and his knees throbbed. The distance between peaks seemed impossibly long. The old days of traveling between cities on foot, even trekking through the mountains, were a long time ago and his feet seemed to have forgotten the ways of the road. Even traveling light, the weight of all that had happened slowed him, and where he used to have exuberant energy for the game of life, now he possessed only a leaden ball in his gut.

When he reached the next peak and found a rock to block the wind, he looked back. The cabin had long vanished into the rocky outcroppings and the snow was falling so thickly that he couldn't even make out the last peak he'd rested on. The world was quickly descending into unending, featureless white, and he imagined that he could spend the rest of his life trapped in it, walking in circles among the peaks until he faded into a ghost and, even then, continue to endlessly wander the valleys, becoming only a myth people murmured about while hunkered down in the darkest nights.

It all made his head feel too heavy to hold up. The enormity of simply walking through the mountains was too much for him, and if his mind managed to think far enough ahead to everything else that was to come, it was enough to make him want to lie down in the snow and wait for it to cover him completely.

Despite it all, knowing that the clouds obscured the sky gave him peace that Sadoc's burning star could not see him. All his life the night was the time that he felt the safest, when he could flit from shadow to shadow and accomplish whatever task he was undertaking. And Sadoc had stolen even that from him, setting his throne as that burning star in the middle of the sky, so no matter what Anuhea did, it felt like the new god was watching everything. And moving across the mountains without Sadoc seeing him was the only thing that made a small part of him inside flutter awake and keep his legs moving. The feeling that he used to have as he began planning a heist, the feeling that he was going to accomplish whatever it was he set out to do and no one would even know he was there until it was over. When the clouds parted, Sadoc would still be looking at that tiny cabin, but it would be empty, and he wouldn't even realize until it was too late.

That feeling could not sustain him for long, though, and when he reached the next peak he descended down into the tree line searching for shelter. Beneath the skeletal trees, the wind and snow was slightly less, but the darkness was still so deep that it took him longer than he wanted to find a shallow cave. He beat the snow from his cloak, kicked the caked chunks from his boots, and went inside. He pulled up snow to cover most of the opening. It wasn't much, but without the wind and fresh snow landing on him, his body heat soon had the area warmer than he'd been since he'd left the cabin.

"Just a little sleep," he muttered to Astra, burrowing himself deeper into his cloak.

When he woke, his head felt like it was a hair's width from breaking in two. Bluish light came through the thin wall of snow he'd pulled up. He pushed his way out, stumbled, fell, retched, and lost everything in his stomach into the snow. A few minutes later, he wiped his mouth and went back for his satchel. Astra was not there, and for a few minutes Anuhea just stood in the snow, staring. The sun was out and anywhere the trees did not cast thin shadows was brilliant with crystalline reflections. The light stabbed his eyes and he started walking with his hand shielding his face, each step heavy and slipping in the snow.

He hadn't gone far when Astra fluttered down and landed on his shoulder.

"You slept for many hours," she said.

Anuhea nodded and paused for a moment as his stomach threatened to try and empty itself again.

"We have a long ways to go," she said. "We need to cover more ground if we are to reach the forest in any decent time."

"Not all of us can fly," Anuhea said. "If we could fly over these mountains, there would be no problems."

Astra was silent for a while before she said, "You need to keep up your strength. Follow me."

She directed him farther down the mountain where the forest had more trees and the ground was thick with bushes beneath the snow. At the base of a tree a hole was visible in the snow. He dug down, and found a small burrow beneath the twisted root of a tree, and huddled in the burrow, snoring contently, were three pikas. Their thickly furred, round bodies expanded and contracted with their breathing, unaware of his presence.

"I've used a little forest magic to keep them asleep," Astra said. "It should be enough for you to eat and have the strength to carry on."

To Anuhea, the idea of the warmth of a small fire and hot meat was the most appealing opportunity in years. Since fleeing into the mountains, he had made do thieving from the small villages in the valleys and from the trappers and hunters who roamed the area and kept cabins and shacks so far away from civilization. Salted meats, cheap ale and cheaper spirits. Dried out, spongy carrots. Stale bread. It had been years of meager meals, and imagining the time next to a fire, the warmth both in the flames and in the meat, seemed enough to almost imagine the old world and the taverns and the comfort.

His hand twitched for them, but he sat back, stared at the animals for another minute, allowed his imagination to continue to run free, and then pushed the snow back up into a mound blocking the view of the burrow.

"I'll forage as we go," he said, turning away.

Astra landed on his shoulder again and said, "I do not understand."

Anuhea didn't look back but stopped long enough to open his satchel. He retrieved the bottle of spirits, pulled out the cork, and took a deep drink. Then another. He exhaled loudly, wiped his mouth, and waited for the warmth in his stomach to reach his head. Some of the stabbing pain subsided, and he had the strength to say, "I can't kill them."

"Your daggers," Astra said. "They will not wake up even if you move them. They are in the deepest of sleep."

"That's not it," he said. He took another drink. "I promised her I wouldn't." He grabbed onto a low branch to pull himself up a slippery slope.

"Promised Tinnu?"

"Don't say her name." Anuhea almost fell. He struggled up a slight incline and found a narrow run of flat land to keep moving north. "Yes." A few more steps. "You said you met her, yes?"

"Briefly."

"Then you might already know. How she wouldn't hurt

anyone." He drank again. "How even as she defended her allies, she did not draw blood. She always found a way through, a way around, a way to calm the fury and a way to escape without causing death." He thought for a minute, walking, calmed by the steady sloshing of the spirits in the jug at his side. "You know the trolls in the deep forest? You never think of them as babies, do you? You only think of them as the giant monstrosities bursting out from the vines, slathering and trying to kill you to cook you."

"The trolls were the death of many elves," Astra said. "Many fine forest walkers found their ends at the claws of trolls."

Anuhea nodded. "She would be the one wondering what a baby troll looked like. She would be the one to wonder if the trolls weren't killing because they enjoyed it, but rather they needed the food for a baby troll to grow up." He paused. "Have you ever seen a baby troll?"

"I have not."

"Can you even imagine one?"

"No."

"Me neither."

"What would be the point? They were savage monsters that killed and ate many of our kind. To show them any kindness would have been the death of countless more."

Anuhea struggled over some rocks, stopped to catch his breath and for a drink. "I used to think so, too." He shook his head. "It was so easy, before. Goblins attacking a village, you go and kill every one of them. No more goblin raids. A necromancer is raising the dead? Find the necromancer and kill him. Werewolves in the night? A silver sword and a talented swordsman puts it all in the past. Pockets filled with gold for the effort. But who out there wept because a goblin went to war and never came back? Who wept because their loved one fell into the dark arts and then a group of adventurers killed him for the reward? Who waited up each full moon hoping that his love would return in the form of a human rather than a beast?"

He stopped to lean against a tree and catch his breath. He shook his head again. "These are all things she thought about. Even as we were tracking Sadoc across the world, trying to stop him from finding all that ancient magic that would let him rip everything apart, she didn't kill anyone. She didn't even draw blood. She was a dead-eye shot with a bow, and yet not a single one of her arrows ever went through something living."

He hesitated for a long time, then started walking again. "She said to me, 'Everyone in this life I've loved has died. How could I do that to someone else? How could I take anyone from them and cause the same pain?' So I promised her. I promised her that I would never kill again. Not an animal. Not a human." He sneered. "Not even a follower of this new god." His fingers were tightened into fists, and it took a long time before he could uncurl them.

"The citadel is filled with those who worship the god that she tried to stop," Astra said. "Not just worship, but follow his commands. They go into the world and kill any who will not worship with them. Any who would seek to live a life different from what they have decided is correct. They have taken everyone from me as well, and I will gladly make them suffer the same fate." Astra was silent for a moment. "It will be impossible, Anuhea, to rescue Ivellios without a death. There will be too many of them. And if you fail, you will suffer the same, terrible fate as every one of my allies."

"I'll find a way," Anuhea said. He said the words, but he didn't believe them. The task before him reared up and was too big and he was too small. He took a drink, trying to make himself feel larger or at least make the world smaller. Some numbness was working into his joints and his fingers. The spirits filled in some of the cracks that made his head feel like it would split. "I'll find a way," he repeated, hoping to believe himself more when he said it again.

Chapter 3: The Avalanche

The sunlight off the snow continued to stab into Anuhea's eyes, but the pain was more distant and dulled. His vision blurred with any sudden movement, and though he was dimly aware that the burning in his eyes was painful, the numbness that had spread through his body made him not care about it. He took another drink from the quickly emptying jug and stumbled down a slope, slipping on the ice before he could dig in his boots, and then stabbing his ankles and shins with the jagged edges. He almost fell several times, his feet sticking in the holes he'd made, but he managed to stay upright as he headed for a low ridge that looked to snake through several of the upcoming peaks. As he descended, the wind lessened as well and he stopped a moment to catch his breath.

"In the old world," Astra asked from his shoulder, "were all of your journeys so plodding and laborious?"

Anuhea chuckled. "Indeed not," he said, and gestured with the jug. "But the human lands were much less mountainous. A journey on a road is much preferable to this constant up and down." He shook the jug and was satisfied by the slosh. "A few more sips, though, and I won't even feel my feet. Then surely I will be able to walk forever and we shall reach our destination in much less time."

He started again, stomping through the icy crust that had formed over the snow. He made it a few steps before his foot caught, tore up a chunk of ice, sent him slipping, stumbling, and finally falling. His cheek grazed the ice and when he pushed himself up, a burn lingered where the skin had been scraped away.

Astra fluttered down, having alighted when he was stumbling. "This is what fifty years does to a legend?"

Anuhea tenderly touched his cheek and winced. "It would be easier if we weren't carrying around such a heavy word," he said. Suddenly the lightness in his body had been replaced by a hollowness and the world was dreary and desolate again. He regained his feet, swayed, but then began trudging forward again. "Besides. Who ever heard of a Wild One being trapped as a bird?"

The juxtaposition of the stories of the Wild Ones and their great magic and the tiny bird hopping aside to not be trampled under his boot was something that would have made him laugh if it didn't seem so sad. He found a shambling rhythm and began to make progress again when Astra landed on his shoulder. They both traveled in silence for a while before Anuhea muttered, "So this is really it, is it? No secret allies that will come to our aid in the final hour? Just an old thief and a bird?"

Astra's toes tightened on Anuhea's shoulder. "The stories that were told about you seemed like you would be enough."

Anuhea scoffed and took a drink from his jug. It chased away some of the bleakness and allowed him to remember the past without having to go through the death and destruction that severed his memory. "Stories, huh? Now there's a grand idea." He took another drink. "A few stories to pass the time. Always helped on the long journeys. Back in the day," he said, smiling and remembering, "I had a great crew to work with." The path sloped down, and Anuhea crouched low to slide down the ice for a few yards. "Had everything you could have ever wanted in a group of adventurers for hire in the old world. A wizard. A swordsman. A dwarf. Did you know that if you had a dwarf in your employ, most of the human nobles would pay you an extra ten percent? They had this idea that dwarves were extra hard working and loyal to anyone who treated them well."

He shook his head, and the smile on his face slowly faded. "Poor old Blaz. If you think I'm a broken mess, you should have seen him when I found him. I hadn't made a proper name for myself in the human lands yet, so I couldn't just go up to one of the established dwarves and ask him to come along as we wandered through the woods chasing off goblins and feral wolves. But I knew that one would give us some credibility that we were lacking, so I was really digging through the back alleys and taverns looking for one willing to come work with us."

Remembering seeing Blaz for the first time gave him an extra weight he hadn't possessed back then. Life had still seemed a game that he was one step ahead of. He'd escaped the sky prisons, avoided being branded a traitor, and had already established himself as a man for hire who would get the job done. Blaz had been just another component necessary to ensure that he could continue to travel across the world without any expectation placed upon him. But in the years since, knowing that Blaz was now dead, and remembering how he had died, left him with only sadness that he had not possessed more to offer the old dwarf when he'd met him. Though the weight of Blaz's death was different than Tinnu's; no matter what, Blaz's past would have caught up with him at some point. At the very least Anuhea had been able to offer him a friendly face as he lay dying. Perhaps, Anuhea had tried to convince himself ever since, he had helped him live longer and find some joy in life rather than drinking himself to death in the gutter. Only in recent years had Anuhea understood the appeal.

"Found Blaz literally sleeping out behind an inn. Right in with the goats. Not because they'd tossed him there. The innkeep hadn't known strong enough men to toss him out there if he had passed out inside. No, he'd just stumbled out there after drinking his way through most of a cask of spirits and that's where he'd landed. The innkeep was happy that I showed up; he was tired of the dwarf getting drunk each night and being belligerent to the other customers. And after seeing the scars on his face and arms, they didn't want to cross him.

"He was reliable, though," Anuhea said. "Dedicated to a fault, so I guess those old nobles knew something I didn't." He walked on in silence for a while, passing into the shadow of one of the peaks. The snow took on a softer shade of blue, but the ice was thicker and harder to break through. Talking about Blaz felt like balancing a thin wall—the memory of the old dwarf was uplifting but the longer he spent remembering, the more risk he took of brushing against the memories that could destroy him. He wasn't sure who he was talking to, anymore. He'd stopped checking to see if Astra was listening, but needed to hear the words out loud.

"He'd been a cleric to one of the dwarf gods back in his homeland. I really can't remember which one. He didn't talk about it much, and at the time, honestly, I didn't think it was that important." Trudging across the ridge, he felt the sudden, insatiable desire to know which dwarf god Blaz had followed. It seemed imperative that he could explain to Astra which one it was, how the tenets of that god had shaped Blaz. But he didn't know, and he realized that while Blaz was alive, he had only thought of him as the drunken, bitter old dwarf he had met in the goat pen and not anyone with a past.

"I guess he'd been caught up in those holy wars. You know the ones, where all those tribes of dwarves turned on each other. I guess he saw everyone he'd ever cared about killed by his own kin. Dwarf killing dwarf far beneath the mountains in the dark. It was enough to make him throw away his vows and leave the mountains forever. I thought he and I were the same, in a way, trying to escape our homelands."

He shook his head. It felt like remembering a different person entirely. Trudging through the snow, thinking of Blaz, it seemed impossible to think that fleeing a homeland awash in blood was anything like his own flight from suffocation. The things that Blaz had seen beneath the mountains were unimaginable at the time, and he knew that, even now, the number of people that Blaz had lost were so many more than Anuhea could count. And there wasn't even a cataclysm to blame for those losses; only religious fervor and long, angry feuds.

Thinking of the religious wars edged Anuhea dangerously close to imagining what Blaz would say in this new world. He drank the last of the spirits in the jug in three quick swallows and pitched the jug away. It shattered on the ice and the shards slid and clattered down among the trees. He stopped a moment, pressed his trembling hands against his sides, and willed his memories away from death and destruction to warmer images.

"Kind old soul," he finally said, and the tremors in his fingers lessened. He started walking again. "Kinder than any of us, though he'd never admit it. I guess there's something to that, isn't there? When everything you've seen is taken away from you, all that's left is either bitterness or kindness. Blaz had a bunch of both, but he only let one show, really."

He remembered that he'd only seen Blaz pray once in all their years together. Mostly, if he spoke of the dwarf gods, it was to curse their names. But after Tinnu had been brought in out of the snow, her hands had been split, raw, and frostbite had been creeping in from the tips. As he walked, Anuhea could only bring himself to remember her hands, disembodied in the darkness, because to remember any more of her was to make him lie down in the snow and wait for another storm to come and bury him forever. The rest of her had been equally mangled, but now, on the other side of everything, knowing how skilled those hands had become with bow and lockpick, there was something particularly haunting about the state of them when they had found her.

Blaz had seen those hands and the shivering state that she had been in. He'd stared at her for a long while as she ate, so long and hard that she flinched away from him the moment he moved closer to her. His gruff voice hadn't helped, but he had seized those hands in his own, strong and callused, and hadn't let go. He'd already been hitting the ale and spirits hard, and his face was red and sweaty, and he was drunk enough that he'd spoken to her in Dwarvish, seemingly unaware that she had no idea what he was saying.

"Listen here, little one," he'd whispered, so low that no one other than Anuhea heard, "I'm going to fix you up. It might hurt for a bit; dwarf gods aren't known for their tenderness. But whatever pain you feel, I'm certain it isn't half of what you've already been through. On the other side, I promise it will be better."

Then he'd begun an old prayer, so low that Anuhea could only catch a few words, and those words were so old and archaic that he hadn't the faintest idea what the dwarf had said. But when he'd released Tinnu's hands, they had been crossed with pale, fresh lines that stood stark against dark tan and dirt streaked skin. Blaz had looked at his work for a moment, then, without saying anything, gone to the bar and remained there, downing cup after cup of spirits until he fell asleep on the stool.

"Which god was it?" Anuhea said. He'd stopped in the snow and was staring down at his hands, shaking and hooked into claws. "There weren't that many of them," he said. "Which one was it?"

"This hardly seems important," Astra said.

"Do you remember the dwarven gods? If I hear the name, I'm sure I'll remember it."

"The dwarf gods were never any concern of mine," Astra said.

"I just need to hear it," Anuhea said. "Did he ever say it? Could we really have been together that long without him saying it even once?"

"There is no point dwelling on the dead when the living are still waiting for us."

Staring at his shaking hands, Anuhea wondered what Blaz could do about the trembling, and the realization he was alone in this journey weighed more heavily on him that he would have ever admitted in the old world. He'd abandoned everything to go off on his own, but after he had met the others, he had come to rely on them in no small way. With each of their deaths, the world became emptier, and now it was full of nothing more than snow and wind.

He looked ahead and back at all the snow and endless peaks. Thankfully, nothing about the whiteness reminded him of the night they had found Tinnu and he was able to move away from the memory. But the memories had stolen the edge of his drunkenness and left him feeling sick. The spirits in his stomach soured, and his tongue felt thick. His head was so heavy that it felt like it was pulling him toward the snow.

His mind snagged on the missing name, and each step seemed to push him farther into the past, trying to remember even a single conversation in its entirety with Blaz. It had been so long and so much had happened that everything was hazy. And the longer he thought about the old dwarf, the more dangerously close he came to remembering his death bed, and that would mean remembering Tinnu sitting at his side.

"He had to have said it," Anuhea muttered. "There were eight dwarf gods, right? Or was it nine? One of them started with a D."

"You should save your breath," Astra said. "None of this will help us enter the citadel."

"No, but having a good dwarf on your team would make a big difference." He wiped at his sweaty face and tried to escape the mire of his memories. "It would take too long, but I don't suppose there's any dwarves in Sadoc's empire that would tunnel into the citadel for coin, are there?"

"A worthless thought," Astra said. "As you said, there isn't time for such a thing, so you are wasting energy entertaining the thought."

"We'll need anything we can," Anuhea said. "What chance do the two of us really have? Even one dwarf with a sturdy shield defending the escape route would increase our chances. Two would be even better. A wizard to spout blasts of fire to keep soldiers at bay would—"

Astra pecked Anuhea's cheek where he had skinned it on the ice. The pain flashed hot and made him stumble. Another vicious peck and he felt the line of blood run along his jaw. "There's no one!" Astra shrieked. She jabbed her beak below his eye, sending him reeling and slipping across the ice. He tried to bat her away, but he lost his balance. Astra flew away as he fell and hit the ice hard. He crunched through the crust and the sharp edges stabbed into his back and shoulders. The fall made the world dizzy and it took him a moment to spot Astra sitting on a branch directly above him.

"Everyone is gone," Astra said. "We have no allies. No elves, no dwarves, no wizards. The world is against us and every second we spend dreaming about things that we can never possibly have is another second that Ivellios slips closer to death."

Anuhea tried to move, but each movement dug the jagged ice in deeper. He winced. "How can you know?" he said. "Dwarves live long enough that there's sure to be a few that are still mad about what Sadoc did to the world."

"I am sure there are plenty," Astra said, "but they will not help us."

"You speak so surely," Anuhea said, slowly dislodging himself and getting to his knees. "Why is that?"

"Because they are enslaved beneath the mountains."

"Enslaved?"

"Every dwarf. In chains in mines harvesting stone and gold to build Sadoc's empire."

Anuhea was motionless for a long moment as his mind tried to comprehend what Astra said. A drop of blood fell off his chin and colored the snow. "Impossible," he said, and wiped his chin. "They're too old and stubborn and loving of their history to give that up. They'd fight. Every last one of them to the bitter end."

"How many of your friends would you see die before you would go willingly? How many of your cities burned with the holy fire from the sky? Can you truly imagine the mines of dwarves burning for a dozen years? While you were hiding, this was their reality.

"Humans rule this world now. Sadoc rules this world. Those who would aid us are hunted down. Killed. Enslaved. Driven so far into hiding that we could never find them. There is no one left who can help us. This is not the old world, and if you are going to go on living in the old world you are worthless to me."

Pushing himself to his feet, Anuhea said, "I gave you my word."

"Your word? What good will your word do if you spend the rest of our lives wandering through the mountains dreaming about the past? You gave your word that you will not kill anyone, and where will that get us? The citadel is full of humans who deserve to die. They will kill you without hesitation at best, put you in a cell and torture you if they can. And you won't kill them? What good is your word against that? What good is your word if you die in that citadel?"

"And what do you have, then?" Anuhea shouted back. "I was done with the world. I'm only heading back to it because of you."

"If the task is too much for you," Astra said coldly, "then you are free to return to your cabin and finish drinking yourself to death. I will go on alone."

"Will you? And what will you do, then? Fly into the citadel and peck every soldier to death?"

"If that is what it takes."

Anuhea scoffed. "No wonder you came searching for a sad, sorry drunk like me. Ivellios doesn't have a hope left in this world."

For a moment there was only the howl of the wind and the whisper of snow across the ice. Then, a faintly whistling whisper from Astra. Anuhea recognized the language and cadence of the language as some form of Elvish, but they were words that were unfamiliar to him.

"Whatever that is," he said, brushing ice and snow from his cloak, "you'll have to repeat it in the human tongue if you want me to get it."

The wind stirred. Anuhea yanked up his hood and started

walking again. A sudden gust hit his back, and didn't abate. The forest filled with sound as the accumulated snow and ice sloughed off the boughs and crashed to the ground, the freed branches creaking and groaning against the wind. Anuhea covered his head against the ice and lowered his hood against the spiraling snow.

He didn't go far before a rumbling made him stop. He looked back to where Astra had been perched, but it was impossible to see anything with all the white in the air. He looked up, and saw the peak whose shadow he was walking through. Snow blew into his eyes and he blinked quickly, thinking the poor visibility was playing tricks on him. It looked like the peak was moving.

He wiped his eyes and squinted and realized it wasn't a trick. The ice crust that covered the side of the mountain was sliding down. Anuhea took several steps back and stared up at the sliding wall of ice creating a fog as it pulverized anything in its path, leaving a blank gray of exposed rock behind.

As the ice and snow dropped off the side of the peak, there was a moment where it fell silently through the air. Anuhea stared at it, slowly backing away, his breath caught in his chest.

When the cascade hit the ground, the entire world shuddered. A cloud of white was kicked up, obscuring the crushing obliteration as the ice collided with the slope above him. The roar of the connection, however, was deafening. The shaking of the ground was so much less than it had been at the breaking of the world, but brought back all the light and all the fear that he'd experienced when he'd watched Sadoc rising into the sky while the rest of the world shattered.

The avalanche was gaining speed and power, but Anuhea could not move. The sun caught the edges of the snowy cloud and filled the air with crystalline sparkles. In each flash of light, he saw the world breaking over and over again, and his fingers hooked into shaking claws. His brain wouldn't work, his body wouldn't move, he couldn't breathe, and all the years of fleeing and waiting and drinking and trying to forget everything had rusted over every muscle, every memory, and to move was to rip through that sedimentation and see again the memories that they covered.

Another second, the wall of ice and snow coming closer, and all those rusted gears snapped into motion. He turned and ran, letting gravity accelerate him down the slope faster than he ever could have moved alone. He slid when his footing slipped, and he saw the steepest way down the mountain. He shifted his path, and within seconds it was less like running and more that his body was falling, but his feet remembered how to slide, how to find a rock, a branch, to control the wild descent. His eyes shot between the path before him and the ground, searching out more footholds, areas where he could slide, where adjustments needed to be made to not collide with a tree.

He glanced back and saw the forest snapping before being swallowed by the rush of ice and snow. It was a wall of white devouring anything in its path and everything it passed over vanished.

A branch slapped against his cheek, but he didn't flinch. He ignored the stinging pain, the burn, and kept moving. What had been a maze of boughs and trunks faded away and Anuhea had a path before him just the way he used to, seeing where his feet needed to go, how he would make it through without having to slow. Just like he'd taught her.

He missed his footing and went down. For a moment all he could see was the snowy ground rushing up to him, but suddenly his shoulder remembered how to tuck itself under his body, how to stay loose and let the rest of him roll over, go with the motion. The world spun for a few rotations, his shoulders and legs and elbows smacking the ground, breaking through crusty ice. More cuts, scrapes, the world moving too fast, his body's spin becoming too erratic to control. He twisted, looking ahead and saw a tree in his path. He twisted again, managed to get his foot under himself, kicked himself back into the air. The tree still rushed at him, but he managed to land on it with his feet. The shock of the impact went up his legs, made his knees strain but the pain was far away. He crouched with the momentum, momentarily sideways, and looked back up the mountain.

The wall of snow was right behind him. Too much in either direction to try and escape, and too close to outrun. He reached up and seized a branch right as his momentum faded and he began to fall. He let himself go limp, let the force of the fall swing him around and he pulled himself up onto the branch. He leapt to the next above his head, pulled himself up, and managed to get one higher before the avalanche slammed into the tree's base.

Anuhea grabbed the main trunk, clung to it with all his strength. The tree shuddered, shook, and he waited for it to be completely uprooted. Break apart like the entire wold had broken apart. The shaking too powerful to do anything but cling. Impossible to move, to advance or retreat. Only wait to see what would happen next.

The snow thundered beneath him. Ice sprayed up and abraded

his face and hands. The world turned white, and each breath was full of frost. He could not see, he could not hear, and the cold sapped any feeling from his skin. The only solidity was the tree, and all around him it seemed like the world was once again fading into nothingness. He felt for a moment that he might be able to pass back through time, and when the snow faded, he would be back in the world before, before he had lost everything.

The rumbling dwindled, much too fast to be the world breaking. The white mist hanging in the air diluted. Slowly, the world returned. Clear blue skies. Behind him, a jagged field of snapped trees protruding from unblemished white. Not even a footprint remained. Looking down, it was like he had not come this way. Nothing behind him, only the new path that would begin the moment he descended from the tree and began to break apart the uniform snow.

All at once, his arms and legs began to shake. His knees throbbed and every cut suddenly burned. His chest ached, and he sucked in huge mouthfuls of air. And there, quickly fading, but lingering like a familiar taste, was a lightness in the air. A purity. A rush of possibility that had existed in the old world.

It took a moment before he could pry his fingers from the bark. His hands were cut and bleeding and each joint ached, but they were steady.

He looked up and saw Astra sitting in the branch across from him, watching him with her depthless eyes. With the last adrenaline of the flight, he looked directly into her gaze and said, "Is that all you've got?"

Already, though, he could feel the trembling returning beneath his skin and knew it would only be a few moments before it vibrated out to encompass each finger, then his wrist, and maybe this time it would continue until his entire arm possessed an uncontrollable quiver. Maybe this time it would encompass his entire body, and he would not be able to do anything except reverberate with the echo of everything he'd lost.

The mountains were filled with silence.

"So," Astra said, "it seems you do still possess some will to live."

Chapter 4: Homeland

Several days later, Anuhea stood with snow crusted in the fur of his hood and thick frozen clumps clotted to his boots on a ridge looking down into a valley cutting into the mountains where they began to peter out and meet the land. Trees crept up the sides of the remaining mountains, and grew into the forest that overran the land and stretched all the way to the horizon. There were no leaves, as if in winter, but the branches seemed to hang darkness in their place. The sun shone clear in the sky, reflecting off the snowy peaks, but something prevented it from touching the forest itself. Anuhea squinted from his high position, but he couldn't see a reason for it to be shrouded in so much darkness.

"It's been a while," he said, "but I remember it being brighter."

He glanced to Astra, but the nightingale remained motionless on his shoulder. He kicked some of the snow from his boots and started his final descent out of the mountains.

It had taken several more days since the avalanche to reach the forest. As the days had gone on, the piercing headaches had ebbed until they were finally nothing more than a dull ache behind his eyes when the sun shone the brightest. Without his heavy head, he moved more quickly, though he had become winded easily. He'd pushed himself through the mountains, forcing his feet to begin to remember the way of long journeys, his lungs to remember how to breathe without ragged gasps.

When he did rest, he focused on steadying his hands. He started practicing with an old heavy coin, rolling it through his knuckles like he used to do when he was bored and waiting. The old familiar motions helped distract his mind, and without his memories eating away at him, his fingers found some of their old fluidity. The movements tired him and he frequently dropped the coin, but that he could even get his hand to steady long enough for a few trips across his knuckles was refreshing.

Knowing that coins would not help him accomplish his task, though, at night he always returned to his daggers. He practiced reversing his grip, switching hands, spinning the blades, and all the old flourishes he used to be able to do with one hand while eating with the other. His fingers were stiff and he frequently pitched knives into the snow, but he retrieved them and continued to practice until there was no strength left in him. Then he slept and continued on the next morning.

While resting, he said nothing, focused entirely on the old practice. While walking, he was formulating what he needed to ask Astra. There were long, stony silences between the two after the avalanche that Anuhea had not bothered to try and broach. But Astra flew up ahead and reported back the easiest paths through the mountains, and he didn't question her. He followed her guidance and focused on his own tasks; he needed to deal with the things he could control before he could begin worrying about what he couldn't. The entire problem of getting into the citadel and rescuing Ivellios was too much as a whole. He knew that if he couldn't even stop his hands from shaking, he wouldn't be able to do a thing and it wouldn't matter how well he planned his entry. There would be time for that later. First, he needed to focus on his own abilities and finding the magic core, facing his old homeland. That alone seemed enough to break him, and he knew that he couldn't break.

Slowly, the aches that settled into him from the road were the old aches that were both familiar and comforting. When he came to a descent, he scanned for an easy path and propelled himself down as fast as he could, leaping from one solid footing to the next, and sliding through the ice and snow when he could not. Going up, he found the easiest paths, the foothold and low branches to help propel him upwards. His hands and feet remembered the movements and slowly began to regain their timing, and his eyes became accustomed to searching through the clutter for the few key pieces he needed; the solid footholds and places where he could slip through unobstructed to move as seamlessly as possible.

As he descended into the valley, the air grew warmer and the ice and snow began to melt from his clothes. There was a difference to Astra's silence now that the forest was in view. She was more statuesque than she'd been, and even as he slipped on some loose stones or stumbled, she didn't alight from his shoulder as she had every other time before on their journey so far.

The closer he came to the first tree, the greater the weight in his chest that something was wrong.

He approached the edge of the treeline and saw that each tree was a pillar of ash. A blackened, charcoal shadow of what they had been before. He reached out and touched it, and the bark crumbled beneath his touch, revealing only dusty gray beneath. He pushed his fingers in deeper, and they were like the cold dregs of a fire in the morning. He jerked his hand back, fearing that if he continued pushing, his hand would go all the way through the trunk. He feared if he pushed, the entire thing would fall as if struck by an ax.

"What is this?" Anuhea asked.

He looked past the young trees at the forest's edge. Not a single, vibrant, emerald leaf hung from a branch, no vine dipped down. The forest floor was devoid of bushes and underbrush, leaving only cracked, gray earth. Even in the afternoon light, the air was filled with flecks of ash and dust, and the trees themselves seemed to suck in the light and create shadows as if the entire forest were shrouded in perpetual mist the color of darkness.

He backed away, as if trying to see all the forest again, but he had seen it from the mountain. All the way to the horizon, the dark trees stretched.

For the first time since he'd left, a flood of memories of his time beneath the canopy came rushing back. Everything he remembered was so diametrically opposed to what lay before him that it had to be a different forest. He glanced at Astra, but she was still motionless on his shoulder. He almost asked if it was the wrong forest, if they needed to travel through some cursed woods and then he would be greeted with the wide river and the thick trunks of his homeland once again. But seeing the trees, remembering Astra's words that there were no more allies, he felt himself go cold despite the warm sunshine.

He pushed back his sodden hood. "Where are the canopies that were so thick you could find night even at noon? The songbirds? Where is the perpetual rustle of leaves caught in unceasing wind?"

"This is it," Astra said.

Ever since leaving his homeland, it had seemed as permanent as a mountain. It would always be there, and there was a sort of comfort in that, even when he possessed no desire to ever return, to ever step foot beneath its canopy again, even if he could. He had been an outsider among the elvish cities, elvish culture, even among the fringes of society where nature and civilization were more fluid. While he lived among the humans, his memory of the forests still existed, and it had always been as vibrant as the day he left.

And here were all the trees again, after all these years, reduced to ash.

"The cities?" Anuhea asked.

"All gone."

"And the elves who lived in them?"

"All dead."

A cold wind blew down from the mountains. Ash drifted from

the naked branches and fluttered through the air like cherry blossoms used to in spring.

"Everyone? No," Anuhea said. He crouched on the ground, and covered his face with his hands, but his fingers wouldn't close over his eyes, and he continued staring into the forest of shadows. His mouth was dry and he wanted a drink. A long slug of spirits to sate his thirst and dull yet another vision of the end of the world. His entire body shook, and he knew that there was nothing to stop the memory from forming, knowing that no matter where he went, the forest of his memory was gone and that anchor—the anchor he had possessed even though he'd never wanted it and hadn't actually cared for it—was suddenly ripped away from him. Without it, he felt adrift, like there was nothing left in the world that he knew, nothing left that he understood, and his mind, untethered, began to swing wildly through all his memories. He could feel his mind approaching the one thing he never wanted to remember, and he began to grasp for anything at all to stop his mind's reeling.

"What of the dragons?" he asked.

"All dead, as far as I can tell."

"The centaurs on the western border?"

"All dead."

"The fairies in the deepest woods?"

"Dead."

"The chimeras?"

"Dead."

"The trolls?"

"Dead."

Anuhea wanted to swat her from his shoulder, but he clenched a fistful of his hair instead. "A single, solitary flower?"

"Nothing."

The air still carried the faint smell of smoke. He stared at the cracked earth, the trees slowly eroding in the wind. "The sky prisons?" he asked, suddenly. Astra didn't answer him.

He remembered back then, to the only time he had been captured and imprisoned. It was the moment that had solidified his desire to escape. Trapped in the hanging cage had been the worst thing to possibly happen. Back then, it was the worst thing he could even imagine. But even then, trapped, unable to move, unable to pursue anything other than remaining in place, there had still been the breeze on his skin. The scent of warm bark. The cadence of rain through the canopy. Butterflies and dragonflies had landed on the woven lattices to rest, and there were always the birds flitting from branch to branch. That had been a scenario he had needed to escape with all his being. He could not comprehend the nightmare before him, with every tree only ash, every animal dead.

"It was elves that stood against him," Astra said. "Elves that followed him across the world, trying to stop him. Elves that came the closest. This was his message to those who would dare to defy him."

Anuhea remembered the ground breaking apart at his feet. The fissure opening wider and wider until, suddenly, far below, there was more sky.

"He would destroy everything just because of the two of us?"

"The fire that rained from the sky was impossible to escape," Astra said. "And it has not only been here. In the early days, after the world split, Sadoc would rain fire down on any who opposed him. It was how he has built an empire in such short time. After a few towns and cities were obliterated in a day, the survivors began to worship him. When they worshiped him, the destruction ceased."

"This is madness. Even for him, this is madness."

Anuhea couldn't stop staring at the trees. He kept waiting for something to move in the old way—a bird to swoop down, a squirrel to dart between two trunks. But the only motion was the drifting specks of ash.

"We have a ways to go," Astra said. "What we seek is west, where the deepest forest meets the mountains."

It took Anuhea a moment to find the strength to stand. When he did, he wavered, almost fell, but managed to stumble forward. When he passed the outermost trees, he looked up, and the sky seemed duller behind the branches. A cold wind blew again, and the sky momentarily vanished, as in heavy snow.

His steps made no sound on the earth, and he heard nothing aside from the wind. The ash fell silently, and there wasn't even the groan or creak of branches. Not a rustle of leaves. He pulled up his cloak to cover his nose against the floating ash, but the smell had already infused in the fur and each breath tasted of old smoke.

As he walked, the trees grew thicker, taller, but they all possessed the same crumbling exteriors. The sky seemed gray and flat from beneath the skeletal canopy, and the silence of the place was so loud that it rang in Anuhea's ears.

"If I could have imagined an end," he said, his voice sounding tiny in the vast silence, "it would never have been like this."

Astra was silent long enough that Anuhea thought she wouldn't answer, but then she said, "This was to be the end if everything in the forest went awry. You know of the story of the sleeping phoenix in the mountains, yes?"

"Vaguely."

"If the time of the elves had come to pass and there was an enemy too great to be defeated, an enemy that endangered the entire world, the phoenix could be awakened and it would reduce the forest to ash."

He looked around. "And where was such a bird fifty years ago?"

"You would have used the phoenix to stop Sadoc?"

"If it was powerful enough to decimate the forest, it would have ended the same way but the world would still be intact. It could have saved everyone."

"Only by killing everyone," Astra said. "It would have been a sacrifice of all to defeat one."

The thought sent Anuhea into contemplative silence. His initial feeling was that Sadoc should have been defeated at all costs, but the longer he turned the thought over in his mind, the more he realized that it was too big a sacrifice. But he also knew that it could have prevented everything, and she would still be alive. The banging back and forth in his head was the exact feeling that had driven him to drink in the first place, and he desperately looked around for something to distract his mind. But all he saw was more desolation.

As the sun descended and the sky took on a hue similar to fire, a dark shape flickered in Anuhea's peripheral vision. He stopped, turned, and his hand was on a dagger. But where the motion had been, there was only drifting ash.

"Are you sure there's nothing left in this forest?" Anuhea said.

"Nothing."

Another flitting, dark shape to his left. Anuhea spun and drew his blade. "And if you're mistaken?" Anything that could have survived such devastation was not something that he wanted to encounter. And if something hadn't been here before, he didn't want to know what type of creature would move into a decimated forest.

"It is nothing. We should hurry."

A whisper just behind his ear made Anuhea spin around and lift his dagger defensively. He drew the other even though there was nothing there. "If it's nothing, I don't see the need to hurry," Anuhea said. He started backing up, keeping both his weapons ready. A low moan like wind made him spin again, but the forest continued to offer only drifting ash.

Then, from behind one of the trees, a black silhouette emerged. It flickered, as if composed of shifting flames in the vague shape of an elf. It lingered for a moment and then vanished. Then, a whisper, in Elvish: "Traitor."

Anuhea kept his eyes where the shape had been, but there was more movement behind another tree farther out. Another shape appeared, as if it pulled itself from the trees like some memory of their burning. "Where were you?" it whispered, though it seemed to be wanting to scream, but simply didn't have the strength. The force of speaking made its form break apart and dissolve into the deepening shadows.

"And what are you?" he asked the forest.

Another materialized beside him, but Anuhea didn't move. He kept his body tense, ready to spring away, but the shape only flickered beside him, not approaching, not retreating. "How dare you return?" it said in a voice like flickering flames.

Anuhea turned to face it, but by the time he'd lowered his weapon, it had dissolved like smoke.

As the light faded, more shapes pulled themselves from the trees, from the shadows, rose up from the earth. They hung in the branches, and their whispers flickered through the remnants of the forest.

Seeing them, hearing their whispers, an old memory of the elf forests returned to Anuhea, and he realized he'd been trying to think of it ever since he arrived. "I remember when I was young," he said to Astra while his eyes flicked over all the shapes materializing and fading, their whispers too weak to fully understand, "we were told that the spirits of the dead would come to you if you went out alone into the forest." He turned his gaze deeper into the forest, toward the tallest trees. "That if you waited beneath an old enough tree, that they would come to you and finally you could have peace."

"The old ways of the forest are gone," Astra said.

"Then what are these?"

"Nothing that will offer you peace."

The light was fading, and the trees looked like they would dissolve into the darkness, and the entire forest would be swallowed up by the night.

"So these are not spirits of the lost elves?"

"This is the agony of the forest."

"What could possibly be here that can help us?" he asked.

"The last of the forest's magic."

"It seems that there is nothing left here."

"The forest's heart still exists," Astra said.

Just behind Anuhea's ear, another shadow whispered, "Thief."

Anuhea spun, but the spirit was already drifting back into the ground. Anhea sheathed his daggers, pulled his cloak more tightly around himself, and hurried along. "The forest's heart," he said. He knew he'd heard of it in his youth, but he couldn't remember anything more than the name. "You make it sound like the entire forest was alive."

"It was."

"I guess you wouldn't be a Wild One if you didn't think that." Anuhea stepped around a black silhouette that stepped out of a tree into his path. "But unless there is some hidden area of forest that wasn't destroyed, I don't know what good a lifeless heart will be to us."

"The tiny shred of magic that remains here is all that keeps these trees from collapsing into dust. If the heart of the forest had truly died, our homeland would be nothing more than an ashen desert."

They passed under a thick lattice of desiccated vines tangled in brittle branches. Spirits pulled themselves all around them, whispering the same word: "Oathbreaker." Their mouths hung open like their jaws were unhinged and kept elongating until they broke off and dissolved into flecks of ash. Their arms reached down and stretched like viscous oil before abruptly breaking apart.

"They can't hurt us, can they?" Anuhea said.

"The forest has lost too much of its life. These are only shadows of what once was."

Anuhea turned and looked at her. "Is this why you're stuck as a bird?"

"I bound my power with that of the forest," Astra said. "When the forest burned, my power went with it. The only form I can maintain is this one."

"You cannot bind yourself to another forest?"

"In time," Astra said. "But it is not something that is done hastily. The forest must trust you, must believe that you wish to protect it, to aid it. If it believes you only seek its power for personal gains, it will reject you."

Ahead, one of the trees trembled, shedding a flaking shower of ash, and then in a whooshing whisper, it collapsed. Ash kicked into the air, and floated across the path, drifted, vanished deeper into the forest. Where it had stood, there was nothing to indicate a tree had ever grown there.

In the distance, Anuhea heard the whooshing of more trees collapsing, the way he used to hear ice sloughing off branches in the winter sun. The light was completely gone from the sky, and for a moment the darkness all around reminded him of the time he had gone far south in the old world, deep into the heart of necromancer land, how even the ground itself had been sapped of all life. As the stars emerged, their light cast everything in vague outlines, and the whispers of the forest became the same as cicadas and crickets from before.

The only star that shone clearly through the ghostly canopy and the drifting dust was the red star of Sadoc's throne. Anuhea paused when he looked up and saw it. Still hanging there in the same place it had for fifty years, still watching over everything that he'd done. Somewhere up there, too far to reach.

He walked through the night, listening for scraps of words from the whispering forest, listening to the distant trees collapsing. In between each, there was silence that was too profound for a forest. It was the type of silence he had sought at the top of mountains, above the tree line, but had been greeted with only howling wind.

Above, the blurry stars spun slowly across the sky around their red epicenter. Anuhea kept his eyes on the ground. Every night, if the sky was clear, Anuhea felt like Sadoc could look down from his throne and see him. Before, darkness had been the time he was most comfortable, slipping from shadow to shadow in the streets or resting by a warm hearth in an inn, full on hot food and cold ale. It was just one more thing that Sadoc had taken from him.

Though he was fatigued from the journey, the constant whispering and devastation of the place made everywhere feel too unnatural to rest. Even if the spirits could not harm him, he feared what types of dreams would arrive if he were to sleep in such an old place full of so much anger.

When the sky began to lighten, Astra directed him to where the forest extended into the mountains in a rounded valley. The peaks towered up all around him, but the forest remained on flat ground. Just as the sun rose and cut through the shadows on the mountains in front of them, Astra and Anuhea arrived at a sheer rock wall.

The wall itself looked blackened, as if the fire that had taken the forest had claimed the rock as well. An archway was carved into the stone, framing a black tunnel. The light from the rising sun shone in a few feet, and inside was smooth and unhewn. The frame was also covered in ash. Anuhea approached, and Astra flitted from his shoulder and perched on a nearby rock. Anuhea went to wipe away the dust to see what was beneath, but the stone itself brushed away beneath his palm.

"This is the elves' most sacred place," Astra said. "Deep in the tunnels lies the heart of the forest."

"So this is what we've come for? In here?"

"Yes. But you must be careful. Originally, it was a place of trials. Few were permitted to enter, and those who did were to be tried to ensure that they possessed the strength and will to use the powers granted within. And among those who have journeyed here, only a few have seen the forest's heart."

"So how do I get it out?" Anuhea asked, looking up at the arch for any hint of what might lie inside. "I can't imagine it will be as easy as just picking it up."

"I do not know."

He turned. "What do you mean?"

"I am not one of the few who have seen the forest's heart. I was among the closest, the Wild One chosen to guide those worthy through the forest's magic to this place so that they might enter. Without me, they would wander the forests forever, lost in an endless web of magic. But I was never to step foot into this place. It is too sacred."

Anuhea nodded. "So only the royal family, then? The queens would come here?"

"No," Astra said. "Only House Nightbreeze."

Anuhea took a step back from the cave entrance. "When she came here," he said, "was this where she went?"

"Yes."

"This was the place that returned her memories?"

"It was."

The cave suddenly seemed more menacing. To walk into it seemed something impossible. "She saw it? The forest's heart?"

"No. She came for different reasons. But all those who pilgrimage here are tested by the forest's magic, and all that they gain comes from its heart, even if they never see it."

Anuhea had the sudden, crazy idea that deep within the forest's heart, Tinnu was somehow still inside. That the entire history of the forest could be contained in it, all its memories. And if he could see the heart, perhaps he could look into those memories and see Tinnu again. Even a faint flicker of her passing among the trees. Even the sound of one of her footsteps.

His hands were sweaty and trembling. He pushed back his hair, drew a deep breath, and said, "All right, then. Let's go."

"Even if the destruction of the world has changed every rule," Astra said, "those rules still exist for me. I am not to step foot in this place, no matter how dire the situation. I was to guide House Nightbreeze to this place, and I was to wait for their return. If they did not return, I was to deliver the news back to the royal family."

Anuhea watched the bird closely. Though he still couldn't easily discern what she was thinking through her avian features, he noticed how she did not look at the cave or the arch. She looked off to the side, back through the forest, as still as if she, too, had been struck down during the world's end and frozen forever in time like the shadows of the forest.

"If I had not come with you," Anuhea said, "you would have had to enter if you wanted the forest's heart. You know that, right? No one else would have been around to do it." He paused. "Would you have done it?"

"What is the point of a vow if you break it the moment a need arises?" Astra said. Her head flicked toward him, but immediately snapped back to the forest. "A vow so flexible is meaningless."

"Even when the only way forward, then, is failure?"

Astra said nothing.

Anuhea watched her for another minute before turning back to the archway. "Well, at least they can't throw me in a sky prison if I mess up this time," he said. He meant it to sound jovial, but he couldn't get his voice right. It came out all wrong.

He walked into the cave.

Within a dozen steps, the light from outside vanished and the depthless black swallowed him.

Chapter 5: An Old Friend

The ground sloped upward through darkness so complete that Anuhea couldn't see even the faintest outline of rock or glint of mica in the walls. He slid each foot forward carefully, unwilling to be surprised by anything as huge as an abrupt crevice or as subtle as a trip wire. There was no telling what might have survived in such a cave, and, like the forest outside, if something had moved in after the entire forest was reduced to silhouettes, he didn't want to announce his arrival before he knew what was ahead.

He reached out his arm to run his fingers along the wall, but found only air. He wanted to look back, to ensure that there was still the glimmer of light back at the entrance, but he feared somehow losing his direction, even if he only rotated his head. The same feeling struck him as he contemplated shifting to the side to find the cave wall. The cave felt old, had the faint denseness that suggested magic lingered in the air. The type of magic that would change the cave around the moment one possessed a shred of self doubt, if any step was taken other than forward. He feared that if he looked for the wall, the cave would suddenly be infinite, and he would never be able to find his way back out of darkness.

Tension coiled through his entire body, like a spring ready to snap, but that quivering balance was familiar to Anuhea. The cave felt like it was still part of the old world, and he had excelled in overcoming the tricks and trials that world had offered. The new world, where a human had become a god and rained fire from the sky onto any who would oppose him, and the elf forest was destroyed along with everything in it, where dwarves had been enslaved and everything and everyone he'd ever cared about were dead, this was the one that troubled him. At least the old world, with all its dangers, was one he had competed against before and always emerged the victor. The singular focus of each foot sliding forward over smooth stone, of his ears ready to pick up any sound that wasn't the scrape of his boots, pushed out all the noise that had filled his head, leaving him with a kind of nervous peace. The danger felt more comfortable than wasting away; moving, even through unknown darkness, felt better in his legs than hiding.

Time fell away and became meaningless. Rushing was the first thing that caused vital details to be overlooked, for everything to go wrong. There was only the feel of each muscle shifting him forward, the silence between each movement. For a moment, he felt he was on just another job, trying to steal something that everyone else had failed to get. All he needed to do was succeed, and he would be flush with gold again and free to travel and follow whatever whim or fancy took him. As soon as he finished, he'd be able to make it back to the inn where his friends were waiting for him. There would be cold ale, hot food, and a fire crackling in the hearth.

Ahead, a faint glimmer of that exact flickering firelight ripped him back from the feeling and grounded him in the present. He froze, because the light ahead was so dim that it seemed like something the cave had pulled straight from his memory. It was too soft, too inviting, and he didn't trust anything that the cave presented to him. He lowered a hand to a dagger and continued his slow creep forward, more conscious that there might be a trap with the distraction up ahead.

The closer he got to the light, the more the cave materialized. He began to see the curve of the rocks, and flecks of mica made the cavern sparkle. After the dead forest, the mica glints were like too-close stars, and Anuhea paused to squint and let his eyes adjust.

The cave turned, blocking his view of the light's source. When he was near enough, he moved against the stone wall so that he could get as close as possible before being seen from whatever was around the bend. He took a deep breath, prepared himself, and peeked.

The tunnel opened into a natural cavern, the rock on the walls subtle bands of tan, gray, and auburn. Everything was smooth, rippled like frozen water, and the light, he saw now, was like that of light reflecting off gently moving creek, not fire, though where the light came from he could not tell. It seemed to emanate from the air, as if the cavern itself wanted to be seen and, if it desired, would snuff it out in an instant.

"It has been a long time since you've been within these borders, Anuhea the Exile," a voice from the cavern said. Anuhea flinched back around the corner, but he had seen no one. He peered out again, and scanned the cavern. It was empty, but the light flickered more rhythmically.

Anuhea thought to run for it, dart through the cavern before whatever spoke could arrive. But he did not know the rules of this place, did not know what to expect if he darted forward rather than waiting and addressed whatever already knew his name. He watched as the light formed into the shape similar to the phantoms in the forest, but the shape continued to define until he could clearly see an elf standing in the middle of the cavern.

All her colors bled into transparent white, everything beyond watery and smeared, like looking through a melting lens of ice. She wore a dress long and flowing, cinched tight at her waist and billowing at the arms and ankles. Her hair was pulled into braids that encircled her forehead and then fell behind her shoulders. Her fingers were adorned with large rings and, despite her incorporeal form, she stood with a firm confidence and her voice carried ancient authority.

"Come into the light, Anuhea the Exile," she said. "There is no use hiding here."

Keeping his hand on his dagger, Anuhea rounded the bend, searching each corner and shadow for hint that there was anything else waiting to spring a trap. The cave's ceiling towered over his head, reminding him of the canopy of trees deep in the forest of old. The cave seemed to be without exit, though behind the spirit there were deeper shadows that even his keen sight could not pierce. "It seems everyone knows who I am these days," he said.

"In this forest, you were once a legend. A ghost. The only one to escape from the sky prisons. There are many who would know your name."

"But not many who would recognize my face," he said. Anuhea watched the apparition closely. In his years since fleeing to the deep mountains to escape the world and his memories, he had rarely seen others, and when he did, they'd all been human. Seeing another elf for the first time in fifty years left him feeling torn between time again, as if he was not in the world where all elves had died. But the fact that she was a spirit spoke to how much had been lost.

"The forest remembers every elf who has trodden its grounds," she said. "Especially the ones that should bear the exile's mark."

"So even with the entire race destroyed, you're still stuck on that." Anuhea shook his head. "Not hard to imagine why I haven't been back, is it?"

"You've returned too late."

"Too late? For what?"

"There's nothing left to save," the spirit said. "The kingdom is destroyed. Our customs survive only in the living memory of the few survivors of our race, scattered across the broken world."

He watched her carefully, and though she appeared to be composed of light, she wavered and flickered at the edges, sometimes more suddenly and harshly, though she continued to keep her chin raised and her shoulders back. Her poise told him she had been part of the aristocracy, and her speech inflection was an even older, more formal version of Astra's speech.

"I'm not here for any of that," Anuhea said. "I'm just looking for a little old magic to repay a debt."

The spirit wavered. "There is nothing left here that will aid you," she said. "The forest is in ashes. The land has been stripped of all life. The world is broken, and no one possesses the power to repair it. And even if the new god was defeated, there are no more Wild Ones to regrow the forest and return it to its former glory."

"There's one."

"Astra of the Wilds?" The spirit scoffed. "Her loyalty to the forest burned down with the trees. Do you not hear the forest's accusations against her? She has betrayed what she swore, and now possesses loyalty only to one. She is no ally of the forest any more. She who the forest saved, she who the forest nurtured when she was cast out, she has forgotten all that the forest gave her in her quest for death and revenge." The spirit looked away. "And even if she hadn't, though she was powerful, once, no single elf can regrow the forest. Even with the forest, our race is destroyed. We will perish. There is nothing here for you, Anuhea the Exile. Had you come before, perhaps your past crimes might have been absolved, but now there is nothing for you."

Anuhea saw that the spirit, though she had once been regal, was worn and tattered. It wasn't noticeable at first, but the hem of her dress was ripped and, farther up, tears showed ethereal knee. Her sleeves bore hundreds of tiny holes, as if moths had eaten away at her for decades. Her hair, at first glance immaculate in its braids, was frayed and split. There was an exhaustion in her eyes, and though her voice was powerful, it also carried a heavy sigh of defeat.

Anuhea released his dagger and straightened. He looked around at the cave, noticed for the first time the cracks running through the walls, the floor. "If everything is going to end," he said, "I suppose you won't miss the last of this place's magic."

"There is none," the spirit said.

"Apparently there is. The heart of the forest."

The spirit flickered like a flame. Its rage wafted off like heat. "So Astra of the Wilds has strayed so far that she has told you, an exile, of it? She would destroy even the memory of this place, solely to save him?"

"I suppose you don't get out of this cave very often," Anuhea said. "There's nothing out there to save. It's already destroyed. It's all gone. And if everything is over already, leaving the forest's heart here will just mean it wastes away. Better to make use of it while it's here than just let it be forgotten and vanish."

"Spoken like a true thief," the spirit said. "It was obvious before that you had no loyalty, no respect for the forest, for what the elves had done here. But even you can comprehend the gravity of what you are planning. If you take the heart of the forest, there is no chance that it will ever regrow. Without the heart, there will never be another sapling sprouting beneath the ash. There will never be another songbird to build a nest on a branch. The trees will vanish and the earth will turn to dust. A desert will replace the once great kingdom of the elves. There will be nothing left. Not even the shadow that you traveled through to get here."

"What good is a shadow of something that was once great?" Anuhea asked. "What is the worth of a forest without birds? Without flowers?" He gripped his left hand in his right to try and stop it from shaking. "You're just trying to hold onto the past. But it's gone."

The spirit looked at his hooked hand. "As if you are any different. Astra of the Wilds would at least destroy this place to save a living elf. You would erase our entire history for a memory."

Anuhea tried to pry his fingers open, but they remained hooked and he hid them beneath his cloak. He looked around the cavern again, trying to find a way out. When he saw none, he said, "As far as I know, there are only three elves left alive. One of them is trapped in a bird's body at the moment, and even if what you say is the truth about her, she has enough loyalty to her old vows to not come here herself."

"Loyalty and vows? Are you a fool as well as a traitor? The heart would not trust her, after all she's done. You are being used."

Anuhea smirked. "Maybe. Whether she could or couldn't come here doesn't change the facts, though. One elf is trapped as a bird, and the other is trapped in a citadel somewhere, being tortured, if he's not dead already. So I'm sure there's some old rule about who the heart of the forest belongs to. Some noble line. But as far as I can see, I'm the only one left of the elves that really has any chance to do something with it. So I'm going to take it."

"You are not worthy of it," the spirit said.

Anuhea shook his head. "If you really know about me, you know that I was exiled for trying to steal the queen's jewels." He shrugged. "I didn't even want them. It wasn't about them as objects. It was that no one had ever seen them, let alone had the chance to take them. No one would have dreamed to try. Everyone loved the queen too much. I wanted the challenge."

He looked up at the spirit and looked straight into her tired eyes.

He saw the fury smoldering there, but he also saw that she possessed no strength. He knew the look, because it was the same one he'd seen in his own eyes for the past fifty years every time he knelt at a pool of water for a drink. "If I was willing to do that for a challenge, do you really think that turning a dead forest to desert is going to haunt me?" He started walking. The spirit began to speak, held out her arms as if to bar his path, but he walked right through her. She was cold, like a wind passing over a frozen lake, but the sensation of his skin frosting over only lasted a second, and he was through her. He walked toward the darkness beyond her, pulling out one of his daggers just in case.

"You're nothing like her," the spirit said.

Anuhea stopped and looked back. The spirit was already fading, more translucent than before. There could only be one answer, but he said, "Who?"

"When she came here, she was ready to sacrifice everything in order to save a land she couldn't even remember. She was prepared to face any challenge, alone, to save our forest. Because it was her duty. Because she was ready to correct the wrongs of her house. And what are you? A loner who would destroy all that remains of her effort, to save her brother? To save one elf, you would erase the entire race from this world?

"She had that chance. The chance to burn this world. Didn't she tell you?"

Anuhea's hand shook, his dagger quivered. His hands were sweaty. "She would never," he said.

"You're correct. She didn't. After all her pain and all her suffering, she arrived here and regained her lost memories of all that had happened to her. Pain that she would never share with anyone ever again. And then, as was her duty, she went and spoke with the phoenix, gone mad with the incomplete ritual her mother began, and the mythical beast offered her a choice. It was her command, the Nightbreeze family right to call upon the phoenix to protect the elf kingdom from the greatest of foes. It offered her the chance to destroy this terrible world and start again, to reduce everything to ash and from the ash would rise new trees, new forests, and, eventually, a kinder, gentler world.

"But Tinnu sided with tradition. She knew the importance of the elves, of this kingdom, and told the phoenix to sleep. To sleep again so that the tradition of the elves, the tradition that had been lost to her for so long, could continue. She chose to keep her own pain so that something larger than her would continue."

The spirit's words crept into Anuhea's heart and made his chest ache. Other than Astra's passing mention, he thought there was no one left in the world who had met Tinnu. And here was a spirit speaking to much about her that he didn't know. His first instinct was to not believe it, but in the time that Anuhea had fled, left her alone, there was much that had happened that he didn't know. It was possible that she knew something about Tinnu that he didn't, that she hadn't told him. She had never mentioned the phoenix, never mentioned much about her time in the elf lands except that she had found her brother.

If the story was true, he didn't doubt that Tinnu would have chosen to save the world over burning it. If anything, it gave more credence to her insistence that Sadoc needed to be stopped, her relentlessness as they followed him across the entire world, always one step behind. After choosing to spare the world once, did she feel a responsibility to saving it?

But Tinnu was never one for tradition. He couldn't think of a single thing about her that hinted, even secretly, that she would have suddenly thrown her lot in with tradition over her own moral compass. Could the memories she found in the elf lands have changed her that much?

He shook his head. "She wouldn't want her brother to die," he said.

"At the cost of everything? At the cost of the forest itself? Would she be willing to make such a sacrifice?"

All Anuhea could think was that Tinnu would, somehow, find a way to save her brother without having to hurt the forest any more. And suddenly he was paralyzed, torn between trying to figure out a way that he could accomplish what he needed without the heart of the forest and also wondering, again, how this new world would have changed Tinnu. His fingers were hooked into claws so rigid they ached, and he wanted nothing more than to pry them straight.

"Why don't you ask her?" the spirit said.

Anuhea felt his body go hollow and sweat broke out across his skin. "Impossible," he said, and his voice sounded far away, as if it didn't come from his own mouth.

"Not here." The spirit waved her arm and some of the darkness dissipated and revealed a keyhole passage in the wall. Anuhea couldn't see anything past the entrance, but its black, empty maw looked like something ready to consume him. "This was a place of powerful magic," the spirit said. "And the veils between worlds are thinner here than elsewhere. Despite the world being rearranged, some old pathways still exist.

"Through there is a place where the dead rest. Just like the old forest, if you wait there with an open heart, they will come to you. And you will be able to ask them the questions that you could not in life."

Anuhea almost dropped his dagger his palms were so sweaty. Everything in his body screamed that it was a trick, a deception of this ancient place to distract him, but he also refused to discount it entirely. If it was possible, even if there was even the tiniest shred of truth to the spirit's words, it would be a place that he would never find in the world again.

As if hearing his thoughts, the spirit said, "Without the heart of the forest, this place, too, will perish. Its magic will dwindle and, in short time, it will be nothing more than an empty cave."

Anuhea stared at the maw in the rock. His brain was empty and he felt pulled toward the place like metal to a magnet. Without glancing back, he moved forward, sheathing his dagger but still moving cautiously. He stepped through the opening and into darkness. The tunnel quickly narrowed, and Anuhea had to squeeze through several narrow spaces where the rocks in the walls pressed out. Stalactites stretched down and he needed to duck and ease past their sharp tips, while stalagmites rose up, some meeting in the middle, but mostly it felt like he was weaving through a long mouth full of teeth. Everything growing ever narrower, more crowded, like being pushed farther and farther back toward some ancient, mountainous throat.

Then, the tunnel ended, opened into a smaller, circular cavern. A thin ledge ran around the room, but the middle was an open hole with sheer walls dropping into darkness. Stretching into the middle of the hole, the path he'd followed extended out a few more steps before also suddenly stopping. Anuhea looked up, but whatever ceiling the cave possessed vanished into darkness.

He crept forward until he was at the hole's center. He knelt down and peered over the edge, trying to see if there was anything on the walls to let him descend. It was impossible to see, and he leaned over and ran his hand along the drop, feeling only smooth stone.

From deep down, a faint whisper. The end of a long echo bouncing between the stone. He leaned farther, straining to hear it. The sound was simultaneously inviting and imperative. He couldn't tell what language it spoke in, but he felt the need to hear it more clearly. He reached down farther, his fingers groping for anything along the smooth edge. He shuffled forward, his boots on the edge, reaching farther down, leaning farther over the emptiness.

"Humph," a deep, gruff voice said behind him. "You cost me a bet."

Anuhea froze because the voice was a familiar one. It was a voice from his past, but so far gone that he had almost forgotten what it sounded like. And when he could place it, it was too impossible for him to believe.

"Blaz?" he said.

A faint whiff of smoke, and Anuhea resisted looking back. It seemed like it would only be some trick, something the cavern had created to deceive him and protect itself. But as he crouched, frozen, there was an annoyed sigh that could only belong to that old, dead dwarf. Finally, Anuhea looked back over his shoulder.

A squat dwarf sat on one of the rough rocks just beside the tunnel, arms crossed and a pipe in his mouth. Broad shouldered, his coppery hair streaked with gray shale falling down and mixing with his beard. His face bore deep creases, and it took Anuhea a moment to recognize him truly. He still had the face of the dwarf who he had found passed out with the goats; not the beardless, gaunt face he'd last seen as his friend died in bed.

Blaz shook his head, swirling away some of the smoke that ringed his face. "I should have known better. I bet you were clever enough to see through the taunts and lies. Thought you weren't stupid enough to fall for some old elf spirit's tricks. Thinking you could actually make it to the land of the dead." He sighed out a thick stream of smoke. "Now not only do I have to pay up, but the rest of them aren't going to let me hear the end of it. They all said you'd fall for it, for certain. That you wouldn't be able to turn away from even the sliver of the possibility that you might be able to see her again. And I was dumb enough to try and defend your moth eaten brain. 'Anuhea wouldn't let his guilt make him that stupid,' I said. And now look at what you've done. They'll be all over it, for certain. You know how they are. And now I don't even have the hope that dying will get me away from their torment. It'll go on forever. All thanks to you."

Anuhea couldn't move. He stared at the dwarf that had died years ago. The first death that had come into his life and stolen away the lightness that inhabited everything. The death that had made things feel like they weren't a game and that he couldn't simply outrun every problem. Sixty years gone, and here he was lecturing him in the same relaxed but condemning tone he'd always possessed. Before his past had caught up with him. Before Anuhea had watched magic poison eat away at his body, watched his beard fall out, and those indefatigable arms wither to sticks. That bellowing voice reduce to a whisper and a wheezing rasp of breath.

It had been the first thing that had made him afraid and made him flee. And everything that followed, everything bad, had been because he had run from that terror, and it was this series of events that he had replayed in his mind over and over again, high in the mountains, listening to the wind and filling his head with stolen spirits.

Blaz heaved out a great, smoky sigh. "But I must have known. Deep down I must have. Because when Tinnu asked me to come here and wait for you, I didn't argue with her. Good thing I didn't, because you'd probably have tried to climb down. Ain't no climbing down that pit, and certainly ain't no climbing back up. One way trip, that is."

Anuhea's mind struggled to keep up with everything the dwarf was saying. "Tinnu sent you? The land of the dead?"

Blaz nodded to the edge of the platform. "Down at the bottom. The path to the place where the dead rest." He sucked on his pipe. "And I know what you're thinking already. Even with me here to tell you what a bad idea it is, you're still thinking about going down there. Trying to just slip in and see them. You really are that dumb, aren't you?"

Anuhea said nothing, because he was looking at the edge and thinking about the land of the dead. How if he could get in, he would be able to see them all again. The whispering wafted up again, and this time he could place the sound better. The general murmur of a tavern on a cold winter night, everyone just come in and not warm enough yet to be boisterous. "Is everyone there?" he asked.

Blaz shook his head. "It's not enough that I'm dead. You're going to make me lecture you one last time, aren't you?" He examined his pipe and tapped it out against the rock. "Aye. Everyone's there." He put his pipe away in some pocket beneath his beard and his hand emerged with a wooden block and a short knife. He exhaled the rest of his smoke out of his nose and started whittling. "But there's no room for you, yet.

"You really can't see this for what it is? It's your biggest temptation. This place was a place of trials, meant to weed out any who were not worthy of possessing great knowledge and great power. Even if the forest is dying, old habits die a lot slower. The spirits here are still stuck in their old ways. So of course they show you the one thing you think you can do: slip into the land of the dead, see everyone you've been missing all this time. Maybe say your apologies. And then slip out to finish your job. That spirit would like you to be in the land of the dead, all right. If you're in there, you can't take the forest's heart and she'll be able to keep on waiting here, until all that magic dries up."

"It wouldn't be the first time I've been in and out of somewhere people said was impossible," Anuhea said.

"Aye. That's true. But there's no coming back once you're in. It's the one place you can't escape from, no matter what."

"But you're here."

He turned the carving about for a few seconds before starting again. "Aye, but I'm not escaped from the land of the dead. I'm still dead. Just momentarily here to help you. Like I told you, this was a place of trials. They have a path for spirits to wander back to this place, but only to help those in need. Fool elves had it so that their ancestors could come and help them, but they didn't make it very well if an old dwarf could find the way here.

"That old hag out there didn't tell you, did she? What they were going to put Tinnu through? A series of trials meant for some elf who'd prepared her whole life to walk through these caverns, guided by an old ancestor who'd passed the trials before, lived to old age to be wise. And there was Tinnu, still too young to know what she's doing, her brain such a muddled mess that she can't even remember the names of the people who tried to protect her when she was young, let alone an ancestor that would know the way through all this mess."

He gave a rough slice and nearly a third of his block clattered to the stone at his feet. "Here's something you can't know, Anuhea. When you're dead, and someone whom you love is in trouble, you can feel it. It comes across time and space and lets you know that they're in trouble, that they need your help. It's not easy to find them, usually, but this place makes it easy. So what do you think I was suppose to do, sitting in the afterlife, and get this feeling that Tinnu is in need? Of course I came running." He looked up with an accusing look, but it quickly softened and he lowered his eyes back to his whittling. "She didn't have anyone else looking out for her at the time.

"So here I am again," he said. He blew some shavings from his hand. "Another elf in a trial he doesn't even know he's in. That old hag out there sure didn't want me coming here, I can guarantee that. She's not being honest in this trial, so I don't think I care much if I'm breaking some rules. I already knew the way here, and someone needed to put you on the right path." He looked up through his thick eyebrows. "You don't have anyone looking out for you anymore, either."

Anuhea looked back to the path leading into the center of the pit. "Why you, Blaz? Why didn't she come herself?"

Blaz silently whittled for a minute. "She's waiting for you later," he said. "When you really need her, she'll come. But if you saw her now, you'd just do something foolish. You're too tied up in the past to think straight. She knew I'm the only one you'd listen to." He inspected his shapeless carving and his thick thumb began pushing the knife again.

"It can't get any worse than this," Anuhea said.

"It will, though," Blaz said. He looked up from his whittling and set Anuhea with a stern look. "You didn't think it would get any worse when I died, but what happened? You came back from your self-imposed exile and necromancers had crept out of the south and were ready to overrun everything you'd come to love in the world. You almost lost Tinnu then. And after she recovered, and the war was won, you thought that would be the darkest moment you would ever live to see. Then this new god comes along and tears the world apart, and everything you love is suddenly ripped away along with it. This is the beginning again. The world still has a lot left to torture you with, Anuhea."

He lowered his gaze back to the wood block. "But this isn't part of all that. This is simple. You just have to walk away, and you've escaped another trap. And even if you did make it into the land of the dead with some way out, how could you look Tinnu in the eye and say anything to her while her brother is still in that citadel? You can't see her yet, because you haven't finished paying your debt."

Anuhea's body sagged, and he felt like he might collapse onto the stone. His body felt so heavy, so weary, and he lowered himself down to the stone. He sat, staring at a spot on the ground just in front of his knees. "You're right," he said. "But even if you're right, it's so painful it hurts. Knowing all of you are right there and I could see you again. But turning away and just leaving. It hurts, Blaz."

Even saying the words made Anuhea's chest feel like it was going to split apart. His hands were shaking so badly that he could barely keep them clenched into fists gripping the edge of his cloak.

"Sentimentality? From you? The world really has changed." Blaz's block kept shrinking, still devoid of anything more than a nebulous, rough shape. "It's not just convincing you to not be dumb enough to walk into the land of the dead," he said. "That's not the only reason I came here."

"No?"

"No. I figured you'd need someone to talk straight to you, since you don't have anyone left. You've gotten slow, Anuhea. Too slow. You think you can get into a heavily guarded citadel and back out with Tinnu's brother in the state you're in? You're carrying around all this weight, Anuhea. The past is stuck in you and you're not going to be able to go forward if you keep looking backwards."

His hands slowed, then stopped. "I know. I know better than the others. That's why I wanted to come talk to you one last time. You've made your choices, Anuhea. You've made them, and things happened. Whether you were right or wrong, smart or foolish, you made those choices and here you are now. Just like when I threw down my hammer and pitched aside my shield and cursed the god I'd followed for a hundred years. Cursed all my kind. All that loss and all that anger was exhausting. You knew it the moment you saw me."

He shook his head and started whittling again. "And here you are doing the exact same thing. You have to put that weight down, Anuhea. If you keep carrying it, you'll be too slow. Too predictable. This new god—he destroyed the world because it was too disorganized. Wanted to make everything systematic. Orderly. That's what this new world has embraced. But you're not part of that world. The only way you'll beat him is to be chaos. The old Anuhea I knew—the one that made me want to pick myself up out of the goat pen and actually do something with my life again—would never allow even a god to catch him."

Blaz opened his hands and the entire block of wood had been reduced to nothing but shavings. He dusted his hands and they all fell to the ground. "So stop trying to fight two battles at the same time. Focus on what's in front of you like you used to. Because we don't want to see you, yet. You have more to do in this world, and you have to do it alone. When you finally lose, we'll all have a party when you show up and we'll mercilessly mock you for your failure. But things take longer once you're dead, so you'd better give us plenty of time to prepare."

Anuhea smirked. "Sounds like a big party."

"Huge. Might take another hundred years to get ready. Maybe two. Better make it two hundred just in case."

Anuhea looked down at his trembling hands, but the small smile stayed on his lips. "I'll almost be as old and slow as you by then."

Blaz reached beneath his beard and took out his pipe again. "You'd better be older and slower. Otherwise you'll have to listen to a new lecture from me every day for eternity. Now doesn't that sound awful?"

"Terrible."

"Good. Now get going, then. You have a citadel to break into and no time to be wasting fantasizing about sneaking into the land of the dead. The Anuhea I agreed to work for would never have fallen for something so simple."

Anuhea shook his head and stood. His hands trembled at his sides. "I don't think that Anuhea exists anymore." Blaz chewed on his pipe. "Thanks for the pep talk, Blaz. I'll be seeing you. Really soon if this heist goes awry."

"I'm already tired of seeing your face," Blaz said. "Already have one elf bothering me. So you'd better do it right."

Anuhea started to leave, but he stopped and asked, "Before I met you, which god did you follow?"

Blaz scoffed around his pipe. "One of the dead ones. One of the foolish ones. But still a right better one than the world has now."

Anuhea started to say something more, but there was nothing in his mouth but the past and dust. He looked at the dwarf, allowing himself to savor the memory of the time before Blaz had died, when they were nothing more than adventurers for hire. Then he straightened, and walked back to the entrance.

When he was next to Blaz, the dwarf said, "Oh, one more thing."

Anuhea stopped, but couldn't bring himself to look at his friend again. "What's that?"

"That old hag lied to you. Tinnu didn't tell that phoenix to sleep out of some loyalty to tradition." Somehow Blaz's pipe was lit again and smoke stung Anuhea's nose. "She chose life. She looked into the eyes of a bird berserk with rage and fury and told it to sleep so that the world could live. She did it so that everyone wouldn't have to watch everything they loved die. She wasn't thinking of the forest; she was thinking of us. Of you. Of every urchin in that city who waited for her to bring them bread. She chose life for herself, living with the pain she carried. She understood why we remember the dead."

"And why's that, Blaz?"

Blaz humphed. "Because the dead had more to say, but they lost their voices before they could say it. The living have to carry their words with them and speak for the dead when its needed. Tinnu was carrying a lot of memories, and she couldn't let the dead be forgotten like that."

"Sounds heavy," Anuhea said.

"Guilt is heavy," Blaz said. "Memory is comforting. Stop looking behind you and keep going forward. You'll remember us when you need."

Anuhea smiled, and it was the first genuine smile he'd had since the world ended. He thought to say something else to Blaz, some parting words, but when he looked to his side, the rock was empty, and only the faintest scent of smoke still lingered in the air. Anuhea, still smiling, shook his head, and walked back through the narrow passage of craggy teeth. He didn't possess any temptation to look back, and when he arrived in the first chamber, the elf spirit was still in the same spot, watching him.

"You're right," he said to the spirit. "I'm nothing like her." Thinking about Tinnu made his smile fade to a small, sad grin. "All that goodness in her, she didn't learn it from me." He looked around the cavern again, and where before there had been thick tapestries of darkness now he could see clearly another exit from the cave. He walked toward it. "Erase everything in this forest to save her brother? I'd turn this place into a desert just to hear her voice one more time. I'd rather have her memory than the chance a new forest will grow here someday that remembers nothing of the past."

"You are a fool," the spirit said.

"Probably," Anuhea said. He walked through the keyhole arch into the next passage without slowing. "But there's not anything out there worth saving, anyways."

After a short distance, he felt a faint breeze on his face. It flew in the sweet smell of amaranths and wet bark. He stopped, the smell having been one he had not smelled since crossing the river to escape the elf lands. Somewhere far ahead, he could hear the faint pattering of rain falling against thick foliage. But it wasn't even that he heard the rain and smelled the forest: it seemed to be an exact rain he had heard once, long ago, and the exact smells he had encountered while walking through the forest on a rainy day. With each step, he didn't feel like he was walking toward a forest, but back into the past itself. Time seemed to brush past him, and he felt the weight of all the years since he'd left begin to lift. He felt lighter on his feet, his fingers surer. In the crevices along the walls, moss crept out, light and wispy at first, but farther along it grew thicker. Tiny clovers sprouted from cracks, and, just at a bend, a white lotus, so pure and immaculate that it was painful to look at.

Beyond the bend, the cave walls sprouted with flowers and thick moss. As he rounded a corner, he flinched back as a butterfly fluttered across his vision. The light in the cave became more and more like the light of the forest on a sunny day. The air was warmer, and soon Anuhea was sweating beneath his cloak.

He rounded a final curve and found himself at the entrance to a massive cavern, but the rocky walls and ceiling were impossible to see. The floor was covered in thick grass and flowers, while the walls were covered in creeping vines and hanging orchids. From the ceiling, thick foliage burst out and hanging moss swayed in wind.

In the center of the cavern, a wooden lattice of interwoven roots arched out of the grass. Beneath the tightly woven layers, a sphere of emerald light pulsed and swirled. The light threw off wind and the thick forest scents of the old forest Anuhea had left behind. The scent of the leaves, of bark, of grass and rich soil poured out of the glowing sphere. There was wind in the cavern, the same breeze that had blown through his cage while he rocked in the sky prison, and, distantly, phantasmal twitters of birds. The creak of branch and the whisper of leaves. It was so much more intricate and lively than the empty, howling winds in the mountains.

Anuhea closed his eyes, and for a moment, again, he was back in the old world. Poised at the edge of the elf lands, hearing the roar of the great river of the southern border, the decision to leave it all behind still light with all the joy of freedom awaiting him. His pack was light, his feet sure, and all the world seemed open and waiting.

The quiver in his hands reminded him, though, that those things had already past. He was too old to be back, and the world had changed too much.

He approached the wooden hemisphere in a wide arc, keeping his eyes on the light glimpsed between the latticework. "And how do you get out of there?" he murmured. Seeing the sphere, he wasn't sure what he was supposed to do. When Astra had first mentioned it, he imagined something tangible, like a crystal. He had stolen enough things in his life that something he could pick up and carry would not be any trouble. However, he had never tried to steal something as ethereal as a sphere of light.

When he approached and rested one foot on the side of the dome, he saw that the light coming from the sphere wasn't all emerald. Mixed in were all the reds and oranges of autumn, the blood-spotted pinks of cherry blossoms, the shocking yellow of a goldfinch darting down from the canopy. The closer he came to the sphere, the more he could hear the forest's old sounds: the light pouncing of deer; snapping twigs; running brooks; the crunch of dried leaves underfoot.

He could feel sunshine on his skin. The air was sticky with pollen, and at the same time chilly like the breeze in autumn. He heard a branch crack and crash to the forest floor in a cascade of ice and snow. He could see the sparkling glints of flakes caught in sunlight buried deep in the sphere's light.

Beneath that light, he caught the glimpse of animals darting about inside.

He circled the sphere for any clue as to how he could get past the thick roots, some hint of a ritual to procure the prize. But he realized that this was not something ever meant to be moved. It was ancient magic, probably forged when the world itself had been born, something that had been here, forming the forest, before even the first elves had arrived. And yet it was also something the new god couldn't have known about. If he had, it would already be gone; destroyed or captured.

"I imagine you already know," Anuhea said, and his voice had the muted quality of speaking in the middle of lush, summer vegetation, "but there isn't anything left outside. The forest is gone." He looked into its light, catching glimpses of woodland scenes flitting by like specks across sight when staring at a bright light. The colors were mesmerizing, and the scenes gave him a sort of peace that he had experienced always believing the homeland he left behind was still standing.

"Do you remember everything?" he asked. "Everything that's happened within your borders?"

He had the desire to scour through every single hole in the lattice, parsing through each color and each shape until he came upon what he sought: the moment in time he had not seen when Tinnu first stepped into the elf forest. Before he could stop himself, he was imagining the scene, and seeing her, even in his memory, made his fingers curl into claws that he could not straighten. He hugged them against himself, but the moment of remembering her made him think about what she would do in this situation. Staring down a sphere containing the sentience of the oldest forest in the world, a thing of unimaginable magic that he needed to save her brother.

But he was certain that she would see the sphere differently, as she always had. She wouldn't see it as a tool to save her brother, even if that had brought her to it. He imagined that the light did indeed remember everything that happened to it. Everything that had gone on, every footstep and every rain. Then: fire and ash.

"You must be in so much pain," he whispered. "And so alone. To have had so long being full of life and now being only ash." He went to gesture, but his hand was still locked into a hook, and he put it beneath his cloak again. "You've lost everything." He tore his gaze away from the memories flitting across the sphere's surface. "And there's no going back to it. Even if you could grow again, Sadoc would never let you. Not something so wild. Something so unpredictable as a forest. That's not his style. Even if he hadn't wanted to destroy everything of the elves, he would have come for you eventually."

He looked up and around the cavern, seeing the tiny fraction of forest the light had wrapped around itself. "You know, there's more of us out there," he said. "People who have lost everything because of Sadoc. People who only have themselves left. And it's easy to rot away in some corner of the world. So easy. So easy to just find a hole and hide in it and wait for death. Dying is so easy." He looked down and looked into the light. "But what fun is easy?"

Anuhea laughed, but it was empty and mirthless, a charade of his former carefree laugh. "Listen. I've made a pretty big promise. There's an elf that needs saving, and I can't really do it alone. I need to fly in the skies, and you might notice I don't have wings. But I know someone who can make it happen if you help. We need a little magic, and apparently you're most of it left in the world. So what do you say? You want to get out of this cave and go make some mayhem? I can't promise revenge—there's a lot of reasons for that and I don't have time to go into them right now. But I can promise that if we survive, we'll be able to make Sadoc really, really mad." His hands began to loosen. "And you'll help me keep a small part of her alive in this world."

He held out his hand and his fingers slowly straightened. "So what do you say? I'm just a lowly elf traitor meant for exile, but maybe that's good enough in this world. I committed great crimes to become free, and that's all I can really offer you. Freedom. Blue skies and a warm breeze."

He laid his hand on the thick lattice. The light flared, blinding him, and when his vision cleared, through the wildly dancing spots, he saw the light creeping out through the holes and up his arm. He stepped back, but the light moved with him, growing brighter, consuming his arm, slithering out of the wooden cage. He tripped, fell, landed in grass and moss, and when he opened his mouth to shout, the light rushed down his throat like water.

Chapter 6: The Journey Through Darkness

In a second, the history of the forest flew through him. He felt each sprouting sapling pushing up through soil and into sunlight, the flickering light of sky passing through sun and clouds and rain and storm. In that moment, Anuhea could see the sky as it used to be, the constellations in the proper places signaling the existence of the myriad gods watching over the world of mortals. Roots spread through the soil, and suddenly there were trillions of insects crawling across his skin, millions of animal feet padding through him, vanishing up trees, leaping from the limbs, taking flight through leaves. And each living creature that called the forest home was an extension of its being, another set of eyes, another sense through which it could perceive the world. Wind and sunshine and rain and snow and the whisper of cherry blossoms carpeting the soil. Everything spreading, multiplying, diversifying, until finally, at the end of the moment, he felt the boots of the elvish patrols along the border. The Wild Ones coming and drawing some of this unfathomable strength, drawing power from the trees and the streams, and using it to expand the forest even further. All of it so quickly, even the longest lived elves were like a blink in time.

Then the sundering.

Agony unlike anything Anuhea had ever felt before. His new, expansive body ripping apart. Roots torn from their trees, the stony bedrock that supported everything cracked asunder. And at just the moment when it seemed that agony alone would be enough to destroy anything, the fire arrived, raining down from the sky like a monsoon. Each new sense served to amplify the pain of fire washing through the forest. A tree reduced to cinders completely through to its core in a moment a different searing than the feeling of charred fur peeling from cooked skin. The great, connecting soil, hardening to blackened clay and then to dust, turning the myriad senses to nothing. In a fraction of an instance, everything was left as ash. The air blew thick clouds of smoke instead of the sweet smell of amaranths and asters.

What seemed ages after the flash experience of millennia, Anuhea diminished back to his normal self, though the feeling of the entire forest remained within him, pressing against the inside of his skin like it would burst forth with the slightest misstep. His skin crumbled like charcoal, and each motion made parts of him flake away and get carried off by an icy wind that wouldn't stop blowing,

He opened his eyes and he was in the dark forest, surrounded by ashen monoliths of the tallest trees; trees taller than anything even in the deepest woods, their branches vanished into the darkness hanging over everything like it was the darkest night. Ash lingered in the air and all the air was gray. It looked like the forest as he had passed through it, but more desolate, yet, more pervasive in its decimation.

Anuhea took a step, and realized there was an incredible weight on his back. The step made his knee feel like it would explode, and he nearly fell. The weight of the dead forest pressed down on him, and there was a silence permeating everything. He looked down and saw his feet sinking into deep ash that sifted soundlessly away as he slid his foot forward, barely able to make the motion beneath his new burden.

He opened his mouth to speak, but more ash rolled from his mouth. For a moment, he feared he had died; feared more that, any moment, all of his old companions would emerge from behind the trees, their faces again pallid, their eyes pearls, their bloated tongues filling their mouths so that they could not speak. He would have to admit to them that he had failed, that he had died too early, but the words would not come out and they wouldn't be able to speak, either. They would just stare at him with those glossy, dead eyes devoid of all the vibrant life they'd possessed. He feared seeing Blaz's bloated, beardless face, and even more, Tinnu's for the first time as only a faded memory.

But aside from the drifting ash, there was no movement.

Anuhea walked, each step feeling like it would force him down beneath the ground. Each step made the forest within him ripple, like water shaken in a jug, and it threatened to throw him off balance, while the decimated forest around him did nothing except slowly pass by. The swishing made him stumble worse than his most drunken moments, those moments when he finally had managed to blot out all the memories. However, the dead trees around him drew all his old memories, like carrion birds circling a wounded, dying animal.

The black lifelessness of the forest took him back to another time in the old world, deep in the south where the necromancers had even sapped life from the dirt. A vast plain of darkness stretching to every horizon. He had walked through that decimated desert, carrying Tinnu on his back, the first punishment for having left her alone.

He tried to wrench his mind away from the memory, to throw

his mind into anything other than those terrifying moments when he looked down and saw her limp hands hanging around his neck, unmoving and twisted from the torture the necromancers had put her through. But the memory etched itself into his mind as permanently as a carving in stone, and it stole the strength from his legs and Anuhea fell. The ash shifted beneath his palms, burying him up to his elbows. He tried to stand, but the weight was pushing him down and his feet slid without purchase.

And this was how he had felt since the sundering. Gone were the days of lightness, the fleet-footed adventures through forest and mountains. It had been how humans had described growing old. He had fled from the world, going higher and farther into the mountains, only using his skills to pilfer food and spirits from villages and trappers. But the truth was that he felt like there was granite in his bones. He felt like he had no movement left, definitely no quickness, and even moving down the mountain to steal enough food to survive another few nights became harder and harder to get started. He had been content to sit in the cabin, in the dark, surrounded by the howling wind, and just wait until there was nothing left.

The stony stasis inside him longed for the earth. Anuhea's arms bowed. He wanted rest. He wanted motionlessness. He wanted to sink into the ground and allow it to engulf him and every memory of the old world.

The ashes brushed against his nose.

A light fluttering near his ear, and a small, ethereal voice sounding like it came from the end of a long room whispered, "Anuhea. Get up."

Anuhea lifted his heavy head. He opened his mouth and the ashes that had pushed in across his tongue fell out. He looked around, but there was nothing different. Just more endless, gray light with shadows of trees. But then there was a new weight on his shoulder, light as a ghost, but the words it spoke were too gnarled and distorted to understand. All he could glean was urgency.

"Tinnu?" he said. "Is that you?"

A whispered murmuring.

Anuhea pushed himself up, stumbled, and caught himself on one of the trees. Ash and soot smeared off on his hand, but he managed to stay upright and draw in several deep breaths. His chest felt like he'd broken all his ribs, and the rest of his body ached as if he'd fallen down a ravine and survived. Time seemed to be solidifying in his bones, and he was losing track of how long he had been anywhere, how long it had been since anything had happened. A creeping dread that he had always been in this ashen forest lodged in his mind and made him waver.

"Walk," the voice implored.

Anuhea took a heavy step. The memory of his previous, weighted march returned. The march through the featureless necromancer lands. He tried to ignore the memory, but it swooped down on him anew and filled his head so completely that he felt he was no longer in the forest but back in that moment. He closed his eyes, and the forest was gone; only the blighted earth remained, stars and moon hidden behind thick clouds so it felt like he walked through nothingness. Tinnu's motionless, broken, lithe weight at his back made impossibly heavier with the weight of his guilt. And at the time, how he had chastised her for forgetting his most important lesson: that she was to be a shadow, passing unseen. "You are not a hero," he'd told her. And the weight of that remorse had grown over the years, compacted down until now the weight of the forest on his back was not the forest but the guilt of what he had done.

Because Blaz had died, Anuhea had fled. He had vanished in the night to try and find a place in the world to hide, a place where he could escape from the reality that those closest to him could be killed. That something as timeless as a hearty dwarf could be reduced to a twig that would break in front of him. To watch his beard fall out, to see Tinnu, one day, crouched at his bedside, crying and holding the thick tufts that were falling out faster than wind could strip a tree in autumn. He had tried to hide from that memory, from that reality, and when he had finally returned, he had learned that Tinnu had made powerful enemies trying to help those in need. She had helped the sister of a necromancer, and, in the journeys he had missed, she had learned enough that they wanted everything she knew. They had taken her deep into their undead empire, and were doing anything they could to draw out her knowledge.

She was his apprentice, so he had gone to get her back. It was the skills he had taught her that had allowed her to help those with such powerful enemies, and the skills he had taught her that had landed her in a necromancer's dungeon. A war waged all around the city, the final war that would drive necromancers again from the land and, everyone believed, make the rest of the world safe. None of it had mattered to him; he had gone only because Tinnu was there.

And since the world had sundered, it was this moment that he always remembered. If he had not fled, Tinnu would not have allied herself with the necromancer's sister; would not have followed her, searching through darkness and learning dark truths. And it was the allies that she made before being captured that helped as she followed Sadoc across the world, trying to stop him. She wouldn't have known what Sadoc was trying until he had succeeded, and at least then she would have survived the sundering. She would still be in this world, and if she hadn't tried to stop Sadoc, he wouldn't have been there, either, and maybe then the elf forests would still be standing.

But imagining her having to see everything destroyed and everyone flocking to worship the destroyer. What would she make of this new, terrible world?

Again that heavy, damning weight on his back. The weight of all his mistakes. Trudging through darkness seemingly without end.

He turned his head, trying to see what was behind him, but just like before, he couldn't see her. He couldn't even feel her breath on his cheek.

"Hey, Tinnu?" he said again, as he had then. "Do you remember the first night we met?" The darkness stretching through the trees was like the darkness that night; the ash floating in the air like the snow coming silently down. "All those cold, hard, perfect flakes."

He remembered the streets were smoothed and unmarked, like the city was completely empty. He remembered the sudden motion out of the alley, pushing back his cloak to grab his dagger, and Tinnu darting in as if she knew that was exactly what he would do. The cloak back, his coin purse was exposed, and she grabbed it and started off. He was too quick, though, and sent her sprawling into the snow. He'd stepped on her arm before she could scramble up and took the sack of coins back.

"Nice try," he'd said, and laughed. "But you're going to have to be faster than that to rob someone like me."

She had followed him, and at the time he'd assumed that she was waiting for another chance to take his gold. He hadn't been worried, and when he arrived back at the tavern where the others were waiting, he'd been ready to shut the door on her, order ales, and recount whatever tale it was that had landed him with a sackful of coin. But his companions had seen her and they'd possessed more compassion than he had. They put her next to the fire, and it was then they saw how bad she was. She must have followed him because she could feel that she was on the brink of death. The bruises and infected cuts and frostbite spoke to one who had never experienced kindness in the world.

Somehow through it all, her own compassion had remained intact. And when she became his apprentice, she studied with a ceaseless curiosity, unending patience to perfect everything he showed her. And despite every lesson he tried to teach her about running away, about hiding, about leaving the world to itself and to only look out for herself, those were the lessons she had not heeded. She had taken his teachings and used them to aid others, and it was that desire to protect everyone around her, even those she couldn't ever have known, that sent her chasing after Sadoc when he was still a mortal man.

"How did you become what you did from what I taught you?" Anuhea asked the weight on his back. "From abandoned in the snow to trying to save the world."

He tried to twist around again, searching for the faint ghost of breath that he had felt before. He nearly fell, the weight on his back different this time, the aches in his body different, and he almost remembered that he wasn't in the past, wasn't walking with Tinnu on his back. But even if the memory was painful, he clung to it, because it was a memory where Tinnu was still there. And as much as it pained him to remember, now that he was so close to her again, he didn't want to wake up from whatever dream or curse had trapped him here. It would be more painful to have to leave her behind again.

"I'm so sorry, Tinnu," he whispered again, pleading with the terrifying potential of death on his back. "I'm so sorry I left you alone. Just when you needed me most, I was gone."

"Would any of it have changed? If I had stayed, would we still have been there, watching the world break, trying to stop a man from becoming a god?"

"Anuhea," the voice implored.

"Tinnu," Anuhea said, "Forgive me. Please. Please."

"Anuhea, breathe."

"Please forgive me."

"Anuhea."

"Please."

"Breathe!"

Anuhea choked. He tried to breath in, but there was something lodged in his throat, his nose, the back of his mouth. He gagged, coughed, and exhaled. He pushed all the air from his lungs, but air kept coming. He felt like he was exhaling everything inside him, and the force of the rushing air felt like it would pull out all of his insides with it, and then his body would implode in on the emptiness. But there was too much rushing out of him for him to stop it.

All around him, the forest shattered, and he felt each jagged piece suddenly inside him and rushing up his throat. The world filled with soot, ash, and soon even the darkness was rushing through him and the world became too bright too quickly. The light terrified him, almost as bright as the sundering world, and then he saw the endless sky coming for him.

Then, there was nothing. No darkness, no light, no sound, and Anuhea fell.

Slowly he became aware of wood beneath his face. A vague hum filled the air around him, like the droning of a million hornets scurrying inside a wall. He tried to lift his head, but he felt emptier than his worst hangover had ever left him. His head throbbed and his bones ached. He managed to slit his eyes open, but the world was watery and full of pulsing green light. He coughed and breathed in, and he could smell the forest.

"Anuhea," Astra said, somewhere behind him. "Rest now. We're on our way."

Chapter 7: The Endless Sky

Anuhea stood on the airship's deck, gripping the railing at the edge, and staring across the endless sky. Wind whipped his hair back from his face, and his jaw and fingers ached from being clenched so tightly. It had taken all of his willpower to make it this far, to step so close to falling, and he didn't have the courage left to look down. He looked left and right, but there was nothing except endless azure and thick islands of clouds. He looked up into more sky, and could faintly see the tiny, hazy red speck where Sadoc sat.

He took a dozen steadying breaths, squeezed his eyes shut, and looked down. A cold sweat coated his entire body and the shaking in his hands rippled up his arms and into his chest. He stood there, quivering, fearing that if he opened his eyes he would see that tiny black speck again, surrounded by falling rock. He opened his eyes and immediately they flicked across everything he could see, and his hands opened, his arms tensed, and he was ready to reach down as if this time he'd be able to catch her.

But there was nothing other than more sky ending in an impenetrable layer of cloud so gray they might as well have been stone.

"So this really is all that's left of the world," he muttered. Staring down into the endless sky, he felt like there was nothing familiar to hold onto and it sent his head spinning. His stomach tried to rise up into his mouth. He had needed to see it, but it was even more expansive than he imagined. The world had become even emptier in the fifty years he'd been hiding away. Before, at least, standing on one piece of drifting land, he could see the others and as he climbed the mountains, in the distance the other pieces were still there, drifting apart, but still visible. And now there seemed to be nothing.

With great effort, he pried his hands off the railing and retreated. The deck was similar to a small ship from the old world, and it didn't take him long to walk to the back. He stayed away from the edge, but watched the direction they came until a large swath of clouds moved out of his line of sight. There, a small mass of land floated in the nothingness. It was so far away that all he could see were swaths of gray and white mountains.

Anuhea had slept for two days, and rested for another two before he possessed the strength to emerge from the ship's bowels. While he lay there he fought against remembering, but small pieces came through. He remembered as the world broke Sadoc rose into the sky and declared that his new world would be full of order. That everything would have its place. That there would be no more chaos.

Astra had explained what Sadoc had meant: he had divided the world into four layers. A layer of mountains and stone; a layer of forests and jungles; a layer of plains devoted to the construction of civilization; and the highest layer where his throne sat atop a tower of obsidian and granite. It had sounded too insane to be true, but here in the endless sky with the land of mountains receding, the reality of it became irrefutable.

Anuhea shook. "A madman," he muttered, and turned to the trapdoor leading into the depths of the ship. He climbed down the ladder, and the hum enveloped him. A sound as though the walls were full of angry wasps. He followed the drone through the narrow corridors past the handful of small rooms and down another ladder into the cargo area. In the center of the open space, he went down one more ladder into the deepest part of the ship, where an area was filled with pulsing green light. The hum was overpowered by the sound of a wind passing through a million leaves and the chirping of birds.

The room was tiny and nearly completely occupied by a crystal case. Inside, the heart of the forest swirled a writhing mass of emerald and moss, tinged with deeper autumn colors. Streaked across its surface, though, were clouds of obsidian and granite, angry roiling lit with occasional, deep sparks like lightning.

Astra was there, no longer a nightingale. She possessed the vague form of an elf, but it was an elf unlike any Anuhea had seen before. Her body was covered in thick patches of moss, some creeping up her neck and across her cheeks. Her hair fell in wild tangles across her shoulders and back, all the colors of an autumn forest interweaving. Occasional protrusions of bark peeked out between the swaths of moss, leaving only a few areas where her deeply tanned skin showed through. Her feet had lost their elven slenderness and had widened into the thick-toed paws of jungle cats.

Anuhea looked at the swirling mass of forest for a moment before asking Astra, "Are you sure everything's okay?"

"Yes," she said. "It is secure in the casing."

"Strange contraption," Anuhea muttered, looking the crystalline cage up and down. Astra had already explained that the crystal took magic energy and converted it into the force that allowed the airship to fly.

Seeing it again, Anuhea thought how Astra had said that the

forest's heart should have so much magic that the ship would fly forever. He slowly walked around the casing, watching the swirls and violent lightning arcs. "I wonder," he said, "if this would let us fly all the way to Sadoc's throne."

The silence lingered until Anuhea had made it the entire way around the crystal and was facing Astra. She didn't look at him, but continued staring into the forest's light with a faraway look in her eyes.

"Yes," she said at last. "This could get us there."

Anuhea's body went hollow and the world retreated, the sound of leaves diminishing to something as soft as a distant creek. His hands began to tremble, and he looked into the light. He imagined seeing that red, burning star in the night sky getting closer, closer, until he could see Sadoc's face, again, sitting on his throne. And Anuhea would be at the front of the ship, his daggers in hand, just waiting for the distance to be small enough to jump.

"Why worry about a citadel?" Anuhea said. "Freeing one elf would be like chipping his toenail. Why not go to where the head is and chop it off?" Another silence that pulled Anuhea's gaze away from the forest's light. He realized his jaw ached, he was clenching his teeth so tightly.

Astra said softly, "Do you have an army, Anuhea? Some legendary weapon to cut through the dragons that circle his throne? Are you fast enough to slip past the angels who have sold their sacredness to avoid annihilation, or the demons who swore allegiance to gain greater power? Those are only the legends that we hear come down, that the new clerics preach to his new followers. What else sits at the peak by his side? What other elder creatures came out of the breaking world and now are enslaved or allied?"

Astra looked at him, but her gaze missed him. She stared at a spot just above his head, and Anuhea realized she was looking up to the next floor, where the empty rooms had once had her allies in them, but now only possessed their empty armor and possessions that belonged to no one.

"Do you think I never had such a thought? That all of us who swore to fight against Sadoc and all who followed him did not possess that exact fantasy? That the moment I thought to collect the heart of the forest, I didn't dream of using its power to accomplish exactly what you're imagining? And yet, Ivellios is the most skilled swordsman left alive in the world, and we still could not defeat the humans serving Sadoc. Even if we had a hundred soldiers as skilled as Ivellios, a hundred legends as renowned and notorious as you, even if every Wild One still existed and the forest thrived at its greatest power, we could not besiege his throne. You have seen what he has done to our homeland, and soon you will see what he has done to this world."

She turned back to the forest and rested her fingers against the crystal separating her from the sphere. Angry, black clouds swirled beneath her touch. "There is no defeating him. All we can do is salvage what little is left. Save those we can, and remember the dead." She locked her gaze with his and in her eyes he saw an animal ferocity. "Believe me when I say that if I possessed the power to burn Sadoc's throne to the ground, I would do so in an instant. If any of his followers were here before me, now, I would kill them without the slightest hesitation. But dying will accomplish nothing. Ivellios must be saved and that is all that can be done now."

Her pessimism sounded simultaneously familiar and foreign to him. That hopelessness, that realization that the greatest enemy could not be confronted—that all roads to him had not simply been blocked, but had been obliterated—had settled deep inside him and infected his heart. Years ago, hearing that there was a citadel on top of a massive mountain, surrounded by dragons and demons and angels, his hands would have itched with excitement. He would have imagined what treasures existed within, what great secrets he could pick up and carry out with him. He would have longed for the challenge, to balance on that knife's edge precipice between success and failure.

He wanted to feel that way again. To look at Astra, scoff, and say, "You can stay here, then. I'll bring you back something when I'm done." But his tongue was as heavy as lead, and his fingers had curled and were stuck again.

"What happened?" he asked. "What happened that Ivellios was captured?"

Astra looked down and then back into the forest's light.

"We were betrayed," she said softly. "One of our own. A trusted officer. Gazed into the endless battle before us and saw only hopelessness. Despair. He wanted to surrender. Secretly sent word to the enemy. Suddenly an undefended iron mine was full of soldiers. All our escapes cut off." She gave a bitter sneer. "He should have known, though, that even an elf betraying his own race is still an elf in Sadoc's eyes."

"And you? I presume they didn't notice a nightingale sitting on Ivellios's shoulder?"

"It is because of Ivellios that I am alive." She looked down at the floor, and when Anuhea followed her sight, he saw a dark splotch in the wood. "Our wizard—her name was Sylphana—was wounded right away, and Ivellios knew that if she died, there would be no more hope for our resistance. He remained behind, fending off the soldiers while the two of us took the airship and fled."

Astra stared hard at the floor, her body so motionless it was as if she had hardened into the core of a tree without wind. "We both knew the war was lost. Even if she wasn't dying, what could the two of us do without the others? All we could do was run, hide the airship, and hide her so that Sadoc would have one fewer wizard imprisoned to fly his airships."

Astra touched the crystal again and another wave of dark clouds swirled around her hand. "We both knew that soon only I would be left. Sylphana wanted to see the elf forests one last time. Even if they were destroyed, she didn't want to die so close to Sadoc's empire. We flew to the border of the forest and she walked right to the edge, sat down under one of those decimated trees, and looked up at the sky.

"And do you know what she said to me?" Astra looked at Anuhea and said, "She was one of the youngest in our group. A real dreamer. Still so full of hope and imagination and wonder at the world. She said, 'Look at that. The moon's gone. Do you think Anuhea stole it again?'"

She shook her head. "Can you imagine, then, off in the forest, a faint whisper on the wind that you had survived? That you were still in the world?" She let her hand fall from the crystal, and the dark clouds thinned. The sudden, bright flash of a cardinal bursting from foliage pierced across the space. "I have no hopes of rebuilding our resistance. But I will also not leave any more to die by their hands. I'll do anything, and ally myself with anyone, if they will help me get Ivellios out."

Anuhea turned his back on the forest's light. It was too distracting, too full of the past and longing. He shook his head to try and clear those memories, to clear the desire of what the endless magic of the forest could make possible. There would be time for such considerations later. First he had his debt to repay.

He said, "It seems both of us owe the dead." He went over to the ladder and started up. "It's time to tell me everything you know. We've come too far to fail now."

He climbed up out of the room and waited for Astra to follow him. When she emerged from the hole, she led the way up another floor and into a room. Inside was darkness until Astra breathed into her hands and exhaled a tiny wisp of the forest's light. She tossed it into the air and it hung there like pollen in mid-fall. She breathed a few more specks around until the room glowed.

A table was covered in maps held down with daggers and candles. The rest of the room was packed with barrels and chests, satchels and pieces of armor and racks of weapons. There was only space to stand, but Anuhea could easily imagine the room crammed with a half dozen elves.

Anuhea took one side of the table, and Astra almost across from him, just to the right of the head of the table. He looked down at the maps, and saw that many were roughly drawn areas of the different layers, and below them were old maps of the old world. A few maps seemed to be trying to figure out which areas of the old world were in which layer, but all of them were fragments and pieces that seemed like they should fit together, but there were too many missing pieces for it to make sense.

"What is it you need to know?" Astra said.

Anuhea pushed some of the maps around. "Everything you can tell me about this citadel. Have you figured out which part of the old world it's built in?"

"We have not. So much was ripped apart and reassembled to be systematic that we haven't been able to place many of the different pieces, except for the forests and mountains. Even the animals and the trees themselves are confused, giving direction to places that no longer exist."

"Unfortunate," Anuhea muttered. "If we were lucky enough for it to be an old human city, I might just happen to know the sewer system."

"We never traveled that far into the third layer, so none of us have actually seen the citadel with our own eyes. Just the legends that the new followers of Sadoc tell. They say that shortly after the breaking of the world, Sadoc dropped indestructible stone into the center of the second layer as a reward for those who had gathered to serve him. They say this is the basis of the citadel, and since that day, they have been building around it ever since. Apparently it did land in the remnants of one of the old human cities, but whether it is a single city or several merged together we have not been able to discern. All we know for certain, though, is that although it has only been a few years, the citadel is already formidable and would most likely withstand the siege of even a large army."

"Luckily we're not an army, then," Anuhea said with a sigh. "If it's still under construction, there should be a dozen holes in their defenses."

"From what we could gather, this is not the case. To see this citadel is to think that generations have been working on it. It is completely locked down. Only those with approval from the church can come and go."

"No chance two old elves are on the list, huh?" Anuhea said, trying to find his lightheartedness, but the words came out through a bitter sneer. "No matter, though. I never intended to walk through the front door. Everywhere has a way in that no one thought about. We just have to look hard enough to find it." He looked up from the maps and tried a grin. "They said it was impossible to get in to see the queen's jewels as well."

"It should have been," Astra said.

"Yes, but there's always a blind spot. Especially when guards change."

"This time you cannot be caught leaving."

He leaned on the table and stared at the maps. Seeing them reminded him of previous heists, of poring over maps and plans, finding the exact way in. But he imagined even if plans for the citadel did exist, they were locked away and not something he could ever lay eyes on.

"You said there are hundreds in this citadel?"

"Yes. The highest in the new order reside there, as well as the heads of his military. Rumor has it that he has one hundred warriors, each blessed with some divine gift, and they are the ones who lead his army and conquer the rest of the world."

Anuhea had a brief flash of imagination. Stalking through the citadel, finding these leaders, these men and women who had sworn fealty to the god who had taken everything from him. Each sleeping soundly, believing their lives were set. A dagger in the dark, a slit throat. One after another. Over and over again, until his retreating footsteps splashed through the halls.

The scene stuck in his head for a moment, and it stilled the tremble in his hands. Vaguely, from far away, his stomach twisted at the thought. Before, he had thieved, blackmailed, and fought off monsters in the forests, hunted down quarries and delivered them to high paying patrons, but he had never been an assassin skulking through the night only to kill someone for coin. But looking back, he knew that his hands weren't clean, either, and at least this time he would be avenging what had been done to the world.

It took a moment for the desire to subside and the tremble to return to his fingers. He tried to start pacing, but there wasn't any room. He picked up one of the daggers from the table and gave it a few simple flourishes to distract his hands and his thoughts. "They need food," he said. "They need water. Someone has to bring it to them. How many wagons are coming and going every day? How many traders and farmers are approved to bring them food?" The dagger nearly flew out of his hand but he managed to snatch it and set it down on the table. "We find one dishonest merchant, and we'll have a way in. Oldest trick in the book; greed is the one hole in every defense."

"Do you really think it will be so simple?" Astra said.

Anuhea looked down at all the failed maps and then around at the weapons and supplies. "Of course not. But we need to start somewhere, and dishonest merchants are always a good place."

He looked up and saw that the moss on Astra's cheek was starting to brown and wither. A strand of her hair that had been deep autumn gold had twisted into the brown of desiccated leaves. Across the desk in front of her, there was a light layer of dust that had not been there when he'd entered.

"Astra?"

She reached up and touched her cheek, and the moss disintegrated, leaving only a pale line on her skin. "My powers are not what they once were," she said. "Being so near the forest's heart grants me some of my old strength, but being even this far away while maintaining this form is exhausting."

Anuhea watched closely and noticed how she leaned on the table, how her entire body seemed to be drooping more and more as their conversation went on. "I would think being so close to the essence of the forest would be enough for you to at least stay as an elf for longer than a few minutes."

"You saw the forest," Astra said. She looked down at the floor, and Anuhea could tell she was looking straight to where the heart of the forest rested in its crystal. "But you are correct. There is more than enough for one elf there. But I tied my magic, my being, to the forest. Its destruction was enough to cripple me forever, but, worse, the forest will not give its power to me easily."

"Because it's so damaged?"

"Because it doesn't trust me."

After a long silence, Anuhea said, "The spirit in the cave said that you only had loyalty for Ivellios."

"It is no coincidence that I am the only Wild One to survive the forest's destruction. All the others were in the forest, trying to save it, as fire rained down from the sky."

"And you were with Ivellios?"

"Ivellios saw that the forest was lost. We sought to save as many as possible to begin our resistance against Sadoc." She looked up and some of her hair broke off like a desiccated piece of ivy. It turned to dust on the way to the table. "No matter what, though, my vows were to protect the forest to the end. And I did not. It is right to be distrustful of me, now. For any magic, even the smallest sliver, I have to prove that I am trying to protect it. That I will not abandon it again." She brushed off some more moss that had browned and decayed on her face. "Though each trickle of magic that it offers me feels more like old habit than the warm bond we once had.

"Perhaps there is still some bargain to be struck. But for the moment, the best I can offer is ensuring the ship stays in the air."

Anuhea nodded even though his stomach tightened at the thought of being held in the air so tentatively. "So once I'm in the citadel, I'm on my own?"

"Yes."

"Fair enough." He looked again at the maps the way he would have done so when they were relevant to his mission. "The more people coming and going, the easier it will be to get inside." He shrugged. "Though that's usually the easy part. Getting back out is what's tricky."

Days passed without much interaction between Anuhea and Astra. Anuhea spent much of his time mulling through the rooms and staring out over the endless sky. The rooms were full of empty sets of armor, weapons without wielders, and dozens of tiny possessions that hinted of an entire group who had come together with shared history but unique lives. A stack of old, yellowed letters. An ink brush painting of a brilliant red bird bursting from a tree. A talisman to one of the old elvish gods whose name Anuhea could not remember. Occasionally he would see Astra standing in the door of one of the empty rooms, simply staring inside. But mostly she remained in the bottom of the ship, whispering in a strange mix of ancient Elvish and sounds reminiscent of wind through leaves and the creak of branches.

"What are you talking to it about?" Anuhea asked.

"I'm asking for forgiveness," Astra said with a tone of obvious regret. But when she spoke again, her voice had hardened. "But also for power. Power to avenge what happened to her. Power to make her enemies pay."

Anuhea thought to ask her about the others, about those who had filled the ship and made it crowded and cramped. But he already felt that there were too many memories in his head, and taking on more to carry around with him would be too many. He needed to focus on the upcoming task, and he struggled to find his easy confidence from before. The more he tried to think about the citadel, the more his imagination found new possibilities, but he had no way of knowing which ones would be actually useful and which were worthless. He knew he needed to see the citadel, but it would be days before they found the continent, and more before they would arrive at the city that had sprung up around it.

With nothing left to do, Anuhea went back to basics. He found and gathered every lock on the ship and spread them out on the floor. He sat with his lock picks, exploring each nook and cranny until he could pop each one open in a few seconds. Then he blindfolded himself and repeated until he could tell which lock was which just by touch. He went into the hold of the ship and arranged the crates and sacks into complicated patterns and practiced running through them, finding the places where he could place his foot to leap and where everything would slide. He made everything unstable, easily collapsed, and tried to regain his lightness and his reflexes. He fell often, slowly accruing a new collection of bruises, cuts, and scrapes.

Occasionally he would be in the middle of a jump from one crate to a pile of sacks when he would suddenly see the world breaking again, see the perfect path of broken earth leading straight up to Sadoc. Every time he remembered, he hit the floor hardest, and had the most difficulty getting back up.

His training of Tinnu had not been much more elegant than a series of boxes and old bags of flour, but he had taken her through the woods, running at a pace he knew she'd struggle to keep up with, and expect her to follow as he leapt from stone to log to low branch, over bushes, and slid through narrow gaps. The freedom of rushing through an area, the focus needed to find each foothold and plan the quickest path through everything, was both joyous and what she needed to learn to escape if she were ever caught in a theft. Trees were more unmovable than people, and were more unforgiving of mistakes.

As he stacked and rearranged each barrel and crate, he would catch himself thinking that he was really designing the course for Tinnu, trying to test a way of movement that she had struggled with. Again and again until she got it right. To shake the feeling, he pushed himself as quickly as he could, and each stumble meant ten more times of perfect execution until he could stop.

When he rested, he practiced his dagger work, spinning them around in his hands and remembering their weight, their movements. As the motions returned to him and began to feel comfortable, he realized that half of the movements were bringing his daggers around for a stab or a cut meant to put his enemy on the ground. Bleeding out. The realization made his fingers curl so tightly that he couldn't undo them for the rest of the day. The next day, he sat staring at the daggers, contemplating the problem, and only after saying out loud, "No one dies, no matter what," could he pick the weapons up again. He practiced new motions that kept his blades flat or turned back, only bringing them into the old motions for parries and blocks.

There was a kind of comfort in revisiting the skills that had rusted during his flight from civilization and his hiding away deep in the mountains. But before they had been a sort of game, a series of fluid motions that were meant to ensure that nothing would take him by surprise and he would always outmaneuver any opponent. Practicing on the ship, with the weight of everything that had happened, felt more like trying to ensure he remembered how to survive. Each movement felt heavier, more final, like it could be the last leap he made, the last parry. The stakes of his goal had never felt higher, even though he was certain there were other more difficult tasks he had been faced with in the past.

When his body was exhausted and his fingers too tired to grip his daggers, he went to the deck of the ship and stared out over the endless sky. It didn't take long for the continent of mountains and stone to vanish into the clouds and only be a tiny speck far off in the blue. He tried to look forward, scanning the horizon for the new continent they were heading toward, but the clouds swirled thick and, no matter what, eventually the entire horizon turned white. He tried to stare into the sky and see only clear blue, freedom. In a way, this was the final realization of his youthful dream crossing the river, leaving behind his homeland. Freedom from every expectation that had been placed upon him. At the time, he had remembered the cherry blossom groves in the capital, and how in spring wind they would dance through the air as if they had not possessed a care, as if they were not even adherent to gravity.

Standing on the deck of the airship, staring out over the endless sky, he thought he should feel like one of those cherry blossoms.

But all he could imagine was the rush of wind pounding in his ears if he fell forever through that blue.

He had never imagined in his life that the things that had once felt so easy would suddenly be so hard.

It had been days since they had left, though the passing of time felt more surreal out in the open sky. The sun never set; it just dipped into the bottom of the sky and cast strange, upward shadows, like the world had turned itself upside down. It was during one of these times when Anuhea was standing on the deck of the ship, hands clamped on the railing and trying to will himself to look down, that Astra emerged from the ship's depths.

She joined him at the railing and looked straight ahead. "There it is," she said.

It took him a minute to find the tiny speck far off in the distance. But once he saw it, he couldn't take his eyes away. Slowly, a new continent grew larger and larger, until it stretched out farther and wider than the view from the highest mountain peak. Seeing it filled Anuhea with dread, though he couldn't quite place where the feeling came from.

"This is the home to Sadoc's empire?" he said.

"It is."

Anuhea nodded, and turned away. "How long until we arrive?"

"A few more days," she said. "Once we are there, hopefully there will be enough trees and birds to tell us where the citadel is. We only have a vague idea from what we could gather before."

Anuhea headed for the trapdoor into the ship. "Time to figure out exactly what we have that will help," he said.

The next few days were spent going through every room in the ship. He started in the hull, taking inventory of what was in every crate, barrel, and bag. Mostly water and foodstuffs, which he'd suspected, but the process of checking everything gave him time to build up his will to begin searching through the rooms above.

When he went to enter the first, he lingered a moment. He could see the blankets piled into four different piles, and he was confident this room had been full of Ivellios's soldiers before their deaths. These possessions had belonged to them, and, though he had never lost any sleep stealing from nobles and ensuring that some of their gold ended up in his pockets, there seemed to be something much more profane about rifling through the possessions of the most recently dead of a nearly destroyed race. The lingering of their spirits hung in the room, and he could tell that Astra was at the end of the hall, watching him.

But with nothing else to aid him, he rifled through each one. In the end, it was nearly a wasted effort. He found a complete arsenal of weapons that he didn't know how to use, full sets of armor that would only slow him down, and dozens of cloaks, boots, tunics, trousers, and brooches. A few thick coils of rope he took and made a pile, as well as most of the blankets and cloaks.

When he had finished, he looked at his meager pile and Astra came up behind him.

"This is it?" she asked.

"Your ship is filled with things for soldiers," he said. "I'm not a soldier."

"How will any of this help?"

"I'm not sure yet." He looked at the ropes, gathered as many as he could carry, and started dragging them to the top deck. "But there are options, at least."

"Not many."

"Sometimes just one is all you need."

He took a rope and tied it to the railing. It took him a few tries to get the knots right, but finally when he yanked back, it didn't slip. He pushed the rest of the rope over the edge and watched the rope tumble, uncoil, and finally jerk straight before gaining a slight bow as it caught the wind. He swallowed back the taste of bile in his mouth and went to the other side.

"Be honest with me, Anuhea," Astra said. "Do you truly think you can accomplish our mission with only what you've brought with you?"

Anuhea silently tied another knot and pushed more rope off the edge. He watched it fall, gripping the railing in a cold sweat. The rope reached a few feet lower than the bottom of the ship. "Good knives and my lockpicks," Anuhea said as he dragged more rope to the back of the ship. "I've done most of what I've done with just those."

"This is different," Astra said. "Everyone will be trying to kill you the moment they see you."

"People have wanted to kill me before."

"An entire army?"

"No, not quite that many." He retrieved more ropes, Astra following behind him. "But I did slip out of the forest with the border guards hunting me. And the queen's guard chasing me." He turned so she could see his clear skin beneath his eye. "I'd say elves were pretty fanatical about branding their traitors."

"This is different," Astra said.

"You'd better hope it isn't."

The day the ship approached the continent, Anuhea was on the deck, watching it turn into a towering wall of rock stretching in every direction. The airship rose higher, and fields of gently rolling grasslands came into view. A tree here and there popped up, but for the most part the entire continent seemed to be flat all the way to the horizon. A river here, a lake there, but the predominate feature was unending, flat plains.

Anuhea rested his foot on the lowermost railing. The wind kept his hair from his face. He watched until the airship had passed out of the endless sky and began flying over solid ground.

"So this is your new world, is it, Sadoc?" Anuhea said. He spat over the edge. He sneered. "I gave you fifty years. I hope you're ready for me."

Chapter 8: The Heart of the Empire

The bustling streets, the shouts of merchants, the creaks and groans of wagons slowly parting the crowds while drivers cracked whips and shouted for everyone to clear way, and the smell of so many bodies crammed together was almost exactly like the old world. When he'd first seen the crowded streets, Anuhea had feared that they would be too packed, too chaotic after spending so long in the mountains, but as soon as he stepped from an alley into the main throng, his feet found their old rhythm and his shoulder remembered how to slip past without jostling anyone. His eyes darted, taking in the movements of everyone in front of him, watching for any unexpected, sudden shifts. He wanted to pass like a ghost through the crowd, so that no one would ever remember that he was there.

Just like he had taught Tinnu.

He kept his head low, his face and ears obscured by an overly large straw hat he'd pilfered from a farmhouse on the way to the city. He and Astra had left the airship floating far beyond the farms and had spent the morning walking through the plains and fields. He'd slipped in and snagged a mismatched disguise from several of the houses, so he looked like a poor farmer with an empty sack either just sold out of his wares or in the city to purchase. The type of person that no one would glance at twice.

It all seemed too comfortable, too much like the old world. Anuhea kept glancing about at all the human faces passing him by, and while he had never mastered the ability to tell a human's age by their faces alone, they all looked like they were young enough to have been born after the world's sundering. Bitter bile rose in the back of his throat as he watched everyone moving about their business almost exactly as they had in those old human cities where he'd found his freedom. That the world could recover and carry on so easily after such a cataclysm would have been unbelievable to him if he were not immersed in it. On top of the mountain, where the howling winds still spoke of the planet's agony and with only icy desolation all around him, it seemed like the world was trapped in the immediate torment the ripping apart of the world had caused. And yet here humans had rebuilt cities, all traces that the world had suffered almost seemed erased.

Anuhea's jaw was clenched, seeing them all oblivious to what had happened. Though he could not imagine Sadoc allowing the history of what he had done to be passed along, the wounds that he inflicted on the world seemed like they should have been irreparable, and he had expected to see only destitution when he arrived in the new world. A city in ruin with its inhabitants crowded together around meager fires sharing stale bread and roasted rats. Instead: carts laden with cabbages and potatoes; cobblers repairing boots and bakers setting out thick loaves.

If he looked closely, he could see small hints of the city's history. Many buildings were built of two different materials; old wood showed frames from long ago and new stone repairs spoke to what had been added afterwards. A few places had buildings nestled so tightly that they had either been built in a flurry or had been pushed together as the earth beneath it was rearranging. A few buildings nearest these packed clusters were crooked, their foundations shifted when the earth flattened or raised. How chaotic it all was made Anuhea smile, realizing how it must irk Sadoc to have so much disorder in his most prized city.

Everywhere, though, construction seemed nonstop. Young men moved about carrying heavy pails of lime and sand, pulling and pushing carts of stone. Buildings were being pulled apart and rebuilt, streets being torn up and new cobblestones put down. As Anuhea moved about the city, it became obvious that the nearer the center of the city where the citadel rose like a mountain, the more the city had been repaired with precise planning. The farther out, the more everything was patched together, the roads uneven and often leading to dead ends.

Slowly, the city was overtaking the old world and applying the new order to everything.

The thing that made Anuhea know for certain that this city was different from the old world human cities was that he only saw human faces. Before, a city this size would have at least a few members of the other races wandering about. A dwarf getting drunk in a tavern or hammering away in a smithy. An elf attending a wizard's academy. A few of the mixed-races as well, so even in a sea of humans there were traces of the rest of the world running through it. But the capital of Sadoc's new empire possessed only humans. Humans in the shops, humans swinging hammers in the forge, humans in the inns, humans haggling with human merchants.

If he hadn't lived in the old world, he wouldn't have even noticed. But knowing the dwarves were gone because they were enslaved in the mountains and the elves because they had burned with their homeland shrouded everything in a maleficent veil. The stones did not pull themselves from the mountains and arrive for building of an empire. The touch of everything that was lost was mortared into each building, embedded in the roads. The humans walking on stones harvested with blood without even a suspicion made Anuhea clutch his empty sack in front of him like a shield and keep his hat pulled low.

He had often passed undetected in the old cities, but not out of fear. He had slipped among the crowded markets, pilfering gold from the aristocracy or eavesdropping on gossip. As he became more famous, there were times he went out disguised so that no one would recognize him, but this was the first time he'd hidden his face because he knew that his face would give him away as an outsider. The face of any elf would stick out in such a place, and even if the people here didn't know or care about the world's sundering, he was certain they knew that the race of elves were considered the betrayers.

Even a random passerby realizing that he wasn't human could create a big enough problem as to ruin any chances he had of getting into the citadel. The only chance he had was that everything carry on as usual and the fortress not be expecting him. If this city was full of followers of the new god, they would not be the ones causing regular trouble, and he needed that complacency on his side.

"What a fetid place," Astra said next to his ear, hidden in the collar of his shirt. "Full of fetid people."

Anuhea didn't respond. He veered near a man dressed lavishly, speaking loudly, and attended by several others carrying heavy baskets and satchels. He grazed against the man's back, barely more than a breath, but his fingers slipped into the loosely tied gold pouch as he did and came out with two coins. He quickly palmed them and carried on, searching for another who looked like he had more than enough coin to spare.

Having completed his cursory introduction to the city, he was working his way toward the citadel, but when he arrived at the market area, he slowed and began mingling. He took his pilfered money and bought bread from a baker and stood near the stall, facing into an empty alley, eating slowly and listening to the conversations passing him by.

Through all the conversations, all the shouts, all the creaks and groans, he realized that there was no song. No bard stood on a corner strumming a lute with an empty tin cup waiting for a stray coin. No taverns had their doors thrown open to let the chants and songs spill out into the streets and draw in passersby.

"I hear they finally caught that elf traitor," a woman carrying a sack of oats said to another.

"Whatever they're doing up there," a man later said to the baker as he waited for his bread, "it isn't too kind to something as traitorous as an elf. May Sadoc bless the rest of those who died trying to capture those rebels."

"So many of our blessed soldiers dead," a young woman said with a shake of her head. "Praise Sadoc that terror is ended."

"Monsters, those elves. Heard they pry the heads off babies and drink their blood. How they live so long, it is. Praise Sadoc there won't be any more of them."

"Hopefully there'll be something worthwhile in that pointed-eared brain of his. Otherwise, he should just be burned at the stake tomorrow!"

Anuhea dusted the bread from his hands and immersed himself into the crowd again. "It seems your little band was quite popular," Anuhea murmured to Astra. He stopped at a stand and bought a bag of apples with his other coin, pilfered a few more from another richly dressed man waiting beside him. He cradled the bag in the crook of his arm and walked, eating the fruit.

Astra said nothing, but Anuhea could feel her quivering on his shoulder.

"I understand," Anuhea said. He looked down at the shining apples in the bag and they seemed too great a thing to exist in such a terrible world. "But we mustn't let our anger interfere with our goal." He looked up at the citadel and his hands started trembling.

It had taken them several days to arrive at the city. Without maps, Astra had consulted the wind and the grass, the few trees, the butterflies and the bees, to find where nature was most obstructed. She followed that pain, sometimes pulled off course by one of the major cities, or to a seam where two chunks of old land had been fused together, but always closer to the citadel in the middle of the continent. These voices, silent to Anuhea, had guided them over gently rolling hills only occasionally interrupted by a lake or river. Farms and villages filled the plains and cities clustered around lakes, but none of them possessed something as imposing as a citadel built on indestructible stone dropped from the heavens.

When they had arrived, there was no need to check that they were at their destination. Rising up out of the city's center was the citadel. Towering walls made of massive gray stones surrounded the central castle, the base of which was stone the color of a starless night. Defensive towers secured each juncture of the star-shaped outer wall. The size of the citadel rivaled the largest castles of the most militant empires he had seen in the human lands before, and the city sprawling out from its center was at least twice as large as any he had seen then.

From the deck of the airship, Anuhea had taken in the city. He could identify most of the areas easily, seeing a clear market district, an area near the citadel walls that seemed devoted to the packed together housing of military barracks. The northern edge of the city was cleared flat, devoid of even grass, where a series of large, wooden airships, similar in design to Astra's but much more massive, sat. Carts and oxen surrounded each ship, and huge sleds laden with stone and wood were being pulled off each.

Roads stretched out in all directions from the city, and it was obvious this was the central hub of Sadoc's new continent-spanning empire. The buildings were predominately made from stone rather than wood, and most of the structures were squat and low to the ground.

Another apple in hand, Anuhea made his way down one of the main roads toward the citadel, instinctively looking down each alley, taking in every shop sign, noting every door that wasn't marked. The bustling streets suggested a city with no seedy underbelly, but he knew that those cities were the ones with the deepest secrets. He was certain every vice still existed, and if he had time, he could find every resource he would ever need. Probably even someone who knew a secret way into the citadel that was reserved for only the most prestigious guests that did not want their comings and goings noticed. But sorting through a city's secret side took time. Even if he had the desire to stay in a city filled with the enemy, risking exposure at every turn, Ivellios did not have the time he would need to sort out such contacts and build plans around new allies. It had taken too long to arrive in the first place, and, though he did not mention it to Astra, every new day increased his fear that he would arrive in the prisons and find the elf already dead.

He had explored the city in wide arcs, unable, at first, to cut straight toward the citadel. But now he made himself walk down the main promenade, watching as it rose up with foreboding impenetrability. The citadel's central keep sat on the only slight hill in the entire city, and even the small rise up to the first wall made everything seem larger than anything humans could ever make.

And it was only being made larger. From the airships came huge blocks of stone, massive trees stripped of branches. On the west side of the citadel, another wall was under construction.

"If Sadoc has everything under his thumb," Anuhea murmured, just loud enough for Astra to hear, "why make something so massive? What war is he preparing for?"

"Not every survivor bowed down, as you can imagine. There were many battles leading to this moment."

"But you said that he holds the world in his grip now."

"This continent, mostly, yes. But what better way to discourage any further resistance than building an impossible to overtake citadel in the heart of your empire? Fear can often do the work of a large army."

A road circled the outer wall, but a glance to the top showed archers patrolling and watching everything passing by below. Anuhea kept moving, trying to look like someone on their way to somewhere else, watching from the corner of his eye. The stones were massive and cut to almost perfectly fit together. As Anuhea walked along one side of the wall, he could see no cracks, fissures, or seams thick enough to fit his fingers into, and he knew that climbing over the wall would not be an option.

The road he followed was wide, with the citadel on his left and a row of fine houses that could only belong to the nobility on the right. Ahead, a junction with another road led to a gate in the wall and a line of men and carts and animals waiting to be let in. Guards in chain and plate patrolled up and down the line and more guarded the gate itself. Anuhea used the movement of the carts to pause and take in his surroundings before passing through the line. It stretched as far as he could see down the road and everything was crawling along. The merchants and farmers were handing papers to guards, and the entire process seemed to take full minutes for each wagon.

If there had been pandemonium, Anuhea would have tried to slip into the citadel among the merchants and farmers. But there was too much time between each wagon, too many eyes watching everything that passed through the gate. Too many guards peering into the wagons, too many shuffled goods to hide beneath them. He moved on, following the road through another line of merchants waiting to enter the citadel, and continued around to the next wall.

As he walked, the large, ornate houses began to dwindle. The buildings shrunk, became dirtier, and soon they became shops and smithies. Carpenters worked in yards, and the ringing out of forges overpowered the other sounds of the city.

Anuhea continued following the road until he found the area that he knew must exist in any city so large. The slums possessed dilapidated buildings clustered close together, some on top of others, some partially collapsed. Men, women, and children lounged in doorways or on the streets, but none stepped foot on the main road running along the citadel. Anuhea looked up at the citadel, realized he was turning along the back wall.

It wasn't long before Anuhea noticed the stench.

Where the buildings were the most dilapidated, a narrow canal cut through the road and continued through the buildings. Anuhea had to block his nose with his sleeve to approach it, though he noticed plenty of people milling about who seemed to have grown so accustomed to the odor they no longer smelled it.

The canal was a few feet deep and filled with slow moving sludge. He glanced down through the houses and shanties along the canal's edge and saw that the creeping liquid continued as far as he could see. Looking the other way, Anuhea saw the source of the river emerging from beneath the wall.

"I guess even citadels need to empty the toilets," he muttered. He crouched down at the edge of the canal and watched the brown liquid meander by. "Do me a favor, Astra. Take some time and fly around and let me know everything you can about what's past these walls. The more you can describe to me the better. Once I'm inside, I'll need to know where the prisons are and how I'm going to get back out."

"You know a way in?"

He looked up at the walls. "Getting in is the least of our worries. I can get in anywhere eventually. But getting out with another elf is going to be a much bigger issue. But we're not walking into that citadel anytime soon to have a look around. So what you can see from the sky will have to do."

Anuhea stood and backed away from the canal. "I'm going to go do some talking. We'll meet back at the airship in the morning."

"Is it safe for you to travel alone?" Astra said. "You are an elf in a city of humans. You'll be easy to spot."

"I know humans better than elves at this point. Besides, it'll take more than any of them have to capture me. If the queen's guard didn't manage it, I'm not worried about a few sentries."

Astra flew out of his hood and it didn't take long before she vanished from sight over the wall. Anuhea stood a moment watching her go, and, despite that he barely knew her, there was a sudden emptiness at being alone again. The gently sloshing in the canal and noise of the distant forges and carpenter saws enveloped him and made him feel like he had been wandering the old city streets. He seized that feeling, tried to forget how the world had changed, and started back the way he'd come.

Seeing the slums told him that not much *had* changed, truly, between the old world and the new. But even more than that, seeing the dilapidated houses, the stench in the air, and the emaciated people huddled around small cooking fires, both for warmth and to share whatever meager scraps they'd managed to acquire through the day, it stabbed into his mind an image of Tinnu that came so quickly he couldn't stop it. There she was again, bending down in her thick cloak, the streets blanketed in snow, a bulging sack open at her feet. "Here," her voice whispered to the form he couldn't see huddled in a lean-to. Only a spiral of her hair falling out of her hood, the tip of her nose. Her hands holding a tough woolen blanket. "Take this."

The image was so strong that he suddenly believed that her spirit was there, still watching out for those that society had forgotten. That she wandered those slums, finding the orphans and delivering bread and blankets to them as she had in the old world. He took a step forward, reaching out for her, almost calling her name. But his fingers seized into claws, and there was nothing in front of him. No snow, no lean-to, and no Tinnu. It was only a memory.

His hands were so locked that his fingers ached. He pulled them close to his body and tried to press them straight again, but they were shaking so badly that he couldn't even get one hand to touch the other to press the fingers flat.

"By Sadoc, mate," a voice said nearby.

Anuhea lunged away from the voice, reaching for his dagger he'd hidden at his back, but his fingers couldn't close on the hilt. His jaw clenched so tightly that it felt like his back teeth would crack, and his eyes were wild and out of focus.

Two younger men and an old man were sitting by a meager fire. "Are you okay, mate?"

One of the men motioned to the ground next to them. "Come here and sit down. You look like you've been through enough and could use a rest."

Anuhea didn't move. He was frozen in mid-crouch, ready to spring into attack or spring away and flee, but his hands were still crooked and his mind was still reeling that he'd gotten so close to a group of people without noticing them there.

"It's okay," one of the men said. "We don't have much, but we have a bit of ale and some bread."

Anuhea's body slowly relaxed. "I've stopped drinking," he murmured.

"Well there's your problem, mate. That'll keep you too high strung. Some bread at least, then."

Anuhea approached the fire cautiously, making an effort to keep his head low and his face obscured by the brim of his hat. He sat down and when one of the men offered him a heel of bread, Anuhea took it with a soft thanks. He handed over the bag of apples and said, "For your kindness."

The two young men nodded solemnly and each took an apple. The one who spoke less pulled a knife from his boot and, after pausing a moment while Anuhea flinched, set about cutting off a thin slice. "Here, old man," he said kindly. "Stranger here brought a gift."

The old man lifted his balding head and looked straight at Anuhea. Anuhea lowered his head under the guise of taking a bite from the bread, and the man leaned forward, intently trying to see his face.

"Old man, take a bite."

"You," the old man croaked.

"He's just a guest. Another poor sod needing a warm fire for a few minutes."

"No," the old man said. He pointed a finger and then clasped his hands. "Oh, no. You. You too."

Anuhea cocked his head to the side.

"You're a ghost."

"A ghost?" Anuhea leaned in closer. "Are there many ghosts wandering around here?" Another flash of Tinnu's outstretched hand, and he was looking all around, trying to catch a glimpse of the edge of her cloak as she vanished around a corner.

"Don't mind him, mate. He's not all together in his head. Old age I guess."

"You're from the old world," the old man said. "You remember, don't you? You remember that sound. That horrible sound."

Anuhea's body went cold. He lowered his head and didn't dare speak.

"Calm down, old man. He's not a ghost. We can see him."

"Oh, spirit!" He tried to crawl around the fire, but the man cutting the apple grabbed his shoulders and pulled him back. "Do you know them? My wife? My daughter? My dear wife. My dear child. Please. Do you know them? Have you seen them? Are they resting?"

Anuhea lifted his head and the man's eyes locked with his. The old man's eyes were watery, and his broken teeth were yellow behind his trembling lips. His lips pulled like he was trying to smile but couldn't get there. "Your face," he said. "I knew it."

"You don't know him, old man. Now calm down. Don't mind him, really."

"I'm sorry," Anuhea said. "I'm not a spirit. Not yet."

The old man went limp in the younger man's arms and began weeping.

"He gets this way some times. He'll calm down in a minute."

Anuhea didn't glance at the younger men. He waited until the old man looked up again with tear-streaked lines through the dirt on his cheeks. "I've seen what you've seen," Anuhea said softly. "Wherever they are, they don't have to hear that noise. Not anymore."

The old man nodded, his fingers gripping the younger man's arms like he was sinking and the man was the only piece of flotsam to keep him above water.

"You as crazy as this old man, mate?"

"Not yet," Anuhea said. He reached into his cloak and took out the rest of the coins he'd pilfered in the market. "Take good care of him," he told the young man. "He's been through more than you'll ever understand." He took the man's hand, placed the coins in his palm, and stood up to go.

"Ghost," the old man choked. When Anuhea lingered, he said, "You too. I can tell. It's written all over your face. Who did you lose?"

"Everyone," Anuhea said. "But I'm going to make it right."

Anuhea left the fire and went back through the streets toward the market. The sun was setting and long shadows crept from all the buildings. He stuck to those shadows out of habit. His head was full of the noise of the breaking of the world, and he struggled to keep track of where he was going. The buildings all began to look the same, and Anuhea finally stopped to lean against one. He squeezed his temples between his palms, and his fingers were stuck into claws again. He drew several deep, shuddering breaths, but he couldn't stop his quivering or get the sound out of his head.

When he finally looked up again, the sky was burnt orange, and the street was filled with people all meandering the same direction. They didn't shove and shout, and the street possessed none of the bustle and noise that it had in the morning when everyone was arriving from the outside.

Anuhea wiped sweat from his forehead, adjusted his hat, and moved onto the edge of the crowd. He followed them through the city, further from the citadel, and more people filtered in from the different, smaller roads off the main one. But he saw where most of them were headed: a cathedral, built of white stone, higher than all the other buildings, with tall windows letting in the fading light.

The sight made Anuhea stop, and the person behind him bumped into him hard enough to nearly send him sprawling. His hands snapped to his head to keep his hat from falling, and he stepped into the shadows of a building to look up at the cathedral.

There had been cathedrals—hundreds of them—in the old world, but they had all been ancient, massive things that oozed history from the mortar. This new cathedral was too large to have been built since the end of the world. He couldn't fathom how it had been constructed so quickly, along with the citadel. He stared at its towers, at the massive archway into its central hall, the massive oak doors, and the sharp-cornered stairs leading up. It must have taken hundreds of men working nonstop for years to make it, and here it was, as if this new world had existed long enough for ancient structures to exist. Seeing the cathedral made him feel dizzy, as if he was suddenly very small and as if time had stretched in some way that he had lost all grasp of it.

Desperately, he tried to remember the fronts of the cathedrals in the human cities, hoping to find one that matched what he looked at. Some old place of worship to an old god overrun with new worshipers, the old holy relics torn down and new ones put up in their place. But he remembered nothing of the white stone, the towers, the way the sun burned in the windows. It was too pristine, the stones too unweathered to be from the old world.

The cathedral represented everything that haunted Anuhea. It rose out of the earth and towered to the heavens in a way that it had no right to. It embodied all that he had lost and all that he had fought against. Seeing the cathedral, he suddenly understood that Sadoc's victory was complete. It was not a new cathedral build among the older structures of other gods; it was the lone place of worship to the only god that remained.

Ivellios and Astra had lost. Tinnu had lost. And there was nothing to glean from all that loss; there was no redemption in their sacrifices.

It was enough to make him sink to the ground and stop moving. The strength went out of his legs and his mouth went dry in the way that only hard spirits could sate. His hands shook so badly he couldn't grab the edge of his cloak to pull about him to fight off the chill that ripped through his body.

The old world was over and gone forever. Seeing the cathedral shattered any possible illusion that he was still in that old world, and that tonight, maybe, when darkness fell there wouldn't be a new red star hanging directly overhead. The weight of all his memories, knowing that he was alone, nearly bore him to the ground.

But he also knew that if he gave up, their memories would all fade. Everyone he had lost would be gone forever if he didn't tell their stories to those still alive. And this world needed them more than they even knew.

Hugging his elbows to keep his hands still, he waited until the line heading into the cathedral thinned and joined the end. As he approached, he noted the height of the doors, the number of stairs, the two guards on each side of the door in plate armor and holding pikes. It was a dangerous place for certain, but he kept his head low and shuffled in behind what appeared a farmer's family.

Inside was high, vaulted ceilings and arches along the sides of the main chamber. Stone benches were arrayed in careful rows, and the best dressed merchants and aristocrats filled the seats. The farmers and the tradesmen stood in the back and in the wings. The central aisle was empty and led to a raised dais, upon which an old man dressed in golden robes stood, his arms outstretched and waiting. On the altar, in the same style as the old world, Sadoc's holy symbol—a lantern sprouting flames that cascaded down and formed a mountain.

But it was the tapestries arrayed behind him that seized Anuhea's sight and didn't let it go. Splayed out behind the altar was an image of the fiery mountain ripping free of the earth and rising into the sky. There it was again, the road of floating debris leading up from the ground straight to the figure bathed in too much light as to be only a watery silhouette.

The man on the dais began to speak, but Anuhea couldn't hear his words. He was focused entirely on the tapestry. With great effort, he tore his gaze away, and saw the other tapestries on the walls. One showed the three pillars in which all the world's magic was contained, ancient structures from when everything was first formed, the structures that Sadoc had sought out across the land and broken to tear apart the world. The pillars that Anuhea had searched for with the others to try and find Sadoc, to get there before him and stop him. Always arriving just too late, even as they triumphed over every delay that Sadoc set behind him.

Then, the breaking of the world.

The rest of the tapestries showed the world being reassembled, each piece being reorganized and rearranged. It was the claim that Sadoc had made, the snippets that they had caught in their infrequent moments when they had caught up with him, only for him to escape again. That the world was too chaotic, and that he would remake it. That he would rebuild the world to make it orderly, predictable. That was it. A madman for order, he had destroyed the world and taken everything from so many, and now there was a cathedral built in his honor, masses gathered to hear about his deeds and worship in his name.

So many battles fought to stop him. So many battles and so much of the world traversed chasing him. Only to arrive as he tore the last pillar in two, ripped it apart and the world with it, deep in the depths of the mountains.

He stared hard at the tapestry behind the altar, scouring the land breaking apart. And just as he was about to turn away, he saw it. Two tiny specks looking up, almost swallowed by the light.

He didn't need to get closer to see if there was more detail. He knew who they were. Even seeing her as a tiny speck, trapped in a building of praise to her murderer, filled Anuhea with a rage that had burned out after the world ended. His shaking hands had a new reason to quiver, and turned and left. He drew stares as he moved, but he made it to the door and bolted down the stairs. He knew that running would draw attention, but he needed to feel the wind on his face. He ran, darted around corners, down streets, away from the citadel and back toward the edge of the city. When he reached there, he kept going, running through the fields and past the chickens and cows until his breath was fire in his lungs and his legs quivered with each step. He stumbled, fell to his knees, and screamed into the dirt road. He screamed again, his hooked fingers digging against dirt and stone.

Panting, he looked back to make sure no one had followed him. No one had. He pushed himself up and began walking back toward the airship.

Night had almost overtaken the sky, and when Anuhea looked up, there was the red star directly overhead, blazing brighter than all the other stars in the sky. The throne of god, visible every night, watching.

Chapter 9: The Citadel

Even after several hours crouching in the darkest shadow of an alley and watching the archers patrol the walls, their pattern had not altered. When one reached the corner tower and turned his back, another appeared on the adjacent wall to cover his sacrificed field of vision.

Around him, the slums slept. Bodies huddled near crackling embers, and there was mostly silence from inside the buildings. The air had cooled, but Anuhea resisted the urge to blow into his hands or stamp his feet for warmth. He kept crouched in his shaft of shadows just beyond a fire's light, shirtless and bootless, one hand gripping his cloak tied up in a tight bundle with his satchel inside.

Overhead, the red star watched everything.

He had thought of a dozen ways to sneak into the citadel. Paying street urchins to harass the guards and create an opening had been one of this first ideas, but he feared that what had once been a common annoyance to city guards would see the innocent children thrown into some deep dungeon, if not for their annoyance in the first place, then surely after he escaped with Ivellios and the citadel realized the children had been a distraction. Anuhea couldn't risk what had happened to the elf forests happening to urchin children.

There hadn't been time to research the merchants coming and going, finding one that could be bribed to sneak him in. Same with the carpenters and workmen who came and went, building scaffolding and hauling stones onto the new wall. Everything had too much risk, and he was certain that, if he succeeded, anyone who had been involved would be put to death at the minimum.

So he had settled on his one last recourse: there had to be a gap in the guards. No guard patrol was perfect. Even the queen's guard of the elves had created a tiny blind spot when they had changed shifts late in the night.

"Patience," he had told Tinnu, early on. "There is always a solution if you are willing to look long enough to find it. No puzzle is impossible."

At first, there had been anxiousness gnawing at his gut. Astra was waiting in the airship and he'd told her to bring it to the top of the northern tower at first light. As he had begun waiting, time ticking by, he knew that each minute that led into each hour was less time he had once he was in the citadel. But he had taken time to steady himself, remember his old lessons and his old successes. Rushing into any situation always created more problems. Often, the easiest solution was to wait.

It was near midnight when the two guards met on the corner tower and stopped. Anuhea tightened his grip on his bundle and tensed his legs. They stood for a few minutes conversing, and then both turned and saluted different soldiers coming up behind them.

Anuhea darted across the road to the wall. He clung to it and ran faster, keeping low. A dozen strides and he was at the canal. He barely slowed when he reached the edge. As he dropped, he looped his arm through his knotted bundle.

He hit the thick liquid with a heavy splat. The muck reached his ribs and he crouched down so only his head was above the muck. Next to him, the open arch in the wall letting the sewage out stared like the open mouth of a putrid beast. Pushing down until his nose was barely above the surface, the stench obliterating his senses, he waded under the wall. He paused just inside and listened for any shouts, any warning that the guards had seen someone dive into the canal. When there was nothing, he moved farther inside and was soon in compete darkness. The ceiling so low that he needed to scrape his cheek along to keep his head above the thick goo he pushed through. He kept one hand firmly on his bundled cloak and the other he felt along the ceiling in front of him. He tried not to breathe, but when he couldn't hold his breath any longer, he turned his lips nearly against the slick stone and drew in tiny gasps.

The air was oppressive, and Anuhea felt like he would lose everything in his stomach if he breathed more than a sliver. The farther he went, the lower the ceiling seemed to get, or the higher the sludge. He could see nothing and could only hear the thick squelching of his own movements through the muck. He kept one hand dragging his bundle behind him and the other pressed against the accumulated slime above him, searching for an opening.

Time seemed to collapse and he couldn't tell if he had been in the tunnel for seconds, minutes, or hours. He didn't want to turn back and see how far the light had retreated for the irrational fear that he would somehow lose his way if he went any direction except straight. Right on the heels of that fear was the realization that he could drown in this filth, and that would be it. Defeated a third time by a river of excrement.

Tinnu and the others would never let him hear the end of it.

He pushed forward with all his strength, and suddenly his hand stopped slipping along the tunnel's roof and pressed up into open air. He immediately lifted his head and gulped in a deep breath, which pushed all the smell down into his lungs. He heaved, held it for a moment, and then emptied his stomach into the filth. He gulped in air, which almost made him repeat the process. Biting the inside of his cheek, he felt around the ceiling to find the side of the shaft above him. It wasn't very wide across, but it was enough for his shoulders and that was all he needed. He looked up, but he was still shrouded in darkness.

Anuhea felt along the walls of the shaft. The walls were dry, and he took a moment to wipe his hands free of muck as best he could on rough sections of the wall. Then, carefully, he probed his fingers along each brick, each crevice, searching for anywhere he could get his fingers into. He wanted to rush, to find a hold so he could get out of the muck, out of the fetid air, and up into the castle and begin his search for Ivellios. But he forced himself to remember his training, remember his patience. For a moment, he could almost hear himself saying to Tinnu, "You went too fast. You went too fast and missed the trick. Try again." He had never rushed into a job, and the careful, systematic probing of all the possibilities had been part of what had allowed him to triumph over all challenges.

Finally, after turning in a slow circle, tracing each brick, he found one that stuck out farther than the rest nearly at the top of his reach. He pressed his fingers all around it, discerning its true size in the dark, and knew it was large enough for his toes. He gripped the brick and pulled himself out of the sludge. Careful to not move too much, he wiped his toes on the bottom stones and pressed each foot against the shaft's sides. When he let go of the brick, his feet slid, the rough stones scraping his skin, but he had enough time to press his hands against the walls and, pressing with all his strength to slow his sliding, he pulled up his foot to catch the protruding brick. Balanced on his toes, Anuhea straightened and leaned against the tunnel's side. He drew in some deeper breaths, squinting his eyes against the smell. His cloak bundle was sodden and dripping and weighed heavily over his shoulder, but he reached up and continued prodding all around the shaft.

Slowly, finding bricks slightly misplaced, cracks and fissures large enough to work his fingers in, tiny crevices to secure a toe and push himself higher, he ascended the shaft one body length at a time, careful with each movement lest he slip and plummet back into the filth. As he went higher, each new body length created a greater realization that a fall would also mean his death. After what seemed like a lifetime, Anuhea reached up and felt a rough stone different from the walls. He felt around it and his fingers went from stone to wood. He pushed. The wood lifted easily. Faint light, barely more than starlight, burst into the shaft, and Anuhea blinked against it. He reached up, seized the edge, and pulled himself up out of the toilet hole.

He fell onto the stone floor with a gasp, his entire body scraped and exhausted. He glanced around and saw he was in a tiny room with an old, moth eaten curtain blocking the entrance. He listened, but he could only hear the sounds of his own breathing. When the throbbing in his feet ebbed, he pulled himself off the floor and peered out one of the narrow windows letting in starlight. The city was a collection of tiny specks of light lining the roads and flickering in windows. Overhead, the sky was clear and all the stars reached all the way to the horizon.

"Still have time," he muttered. He went over to the curtain and peered out, finding an empty hallway. He pulled the curtain down and started to wipe the slime from his body, but he noticed at the end of the hall, barely illuminated by the faint light of one lone lantern hanging next to the archway leading to stairs was a tapestry. A lantern spitting fire and forming into a mountain of flames. Sadoc's holy lantern to drive back the darkness. Anuhea let the curtain drop and went down the hall. He pulled down the tapestry and carried it back with him, wiping at the filth as he went.

The smell of the canal still hung around him, and no matter what he did there was still a film across his entire body that couldn't be scrubbed away. Back in the latrine, he undid his cloak and opened his leather satchel. Inside the satchel had remained dry, though the outside was shiny slick with sewage. Anuhea ensured all his tools were spotless and then peeled off his sodden trousers and dressed in a dry set of clothes. He checked his tools one more time, tucked his leather bundle into his belt, and strapped his daggers to his thighs. When he was done, he stuffed all the soiled clothes and tapestry back down the latrine.

Anuhea stood still a moment, his eyes closed, listening to the silence. He imagined it seeping into him, infusing every hollow of his body until he was part of it. He visualized his steps being silent, and gripped his hands to mitigate their trembling. "Focus," he had told Tinnu. "Don't move until you're ready. Stay hidden until you can move without anyone knowing."

He opened his eyes and went down the hall, moving swiftly but keeping on the balls of his feet. He kept one hand out in front of him, trailing the wall, the other around the hilt of a dagger.

The torch at the end of the hall illuminated the entrance to a tightly spiraled staircase leading down. It quickly vanished into darkness, and Anuhea went on without the light. If anyone was coming up, he wanted to know they were coming and make a retreat. All his senses were so focused his body felt like it was humming. It was the feeling that he had lived for before, and he needed all his focus to hold onto the feeling. Any footstep he wanted to hear. Any flicker of light he wanted to see. His nose was clogged with the stench of the canal, and it made him feel like he would miss some scent and it would lead to disaster. All his muscles quivered with anticipation.

The stairs passed an exit onto the ramparts. Anuhea peered out and saw the guards patrolling between torches set behind crenelations. They moved with the same, steady sureness he had observed half the night already, and it told him that no one was aware he had arrived. That he had already come this far successfully gave him confidence that he could finish the job.

Across the courtyard were the main doors to the keep. Getting there would be the easy part. It was inside that had him worried. He couldn't be sure if that would even be where the dungeons were located, but he figured that they would keep a prisoner like Ivellios in the deepest, hardest to reach part of the citadel. Humans always wanted to lock people away in the dark.

He reached the bottom of the tower and lingered again, watching the guards' patrols on the ramparts, ensuring that they hadn't changed. He watched long enough to ensure that they were concerned with what was happening on the street beyond the walls and not what was happening in the courtyard.

The large open area was the first of Anuhea's big concerns. It would only take one guard to turn around and happen to see him. But he needed to take some risks or the task would be impossible. He reasoned that guards in the heart of Sadoc's empire would be loyal but set in routine. He needed to exploit those routines to slip inside, and that they had no reason to check the courtyard in the dead of night was one hope.

Though he didn't plan on running straight to the door. Tucked against the east wall was a long building that Astra had told him were the stables. It was about halfway to the keep's entrance, and exactly where he wanted to go.

He left the shadows of the doorway and darted to the shadows at the base of the wall. He hurried along, his footsteps silenced in the grass. He listened, catching the scrape of the guard's boots against stone above him, the faint whisper of the wind in the grass. There was a dim light coming from the entrance of the stables, and as he neared, he could hear voices. He crept up beside the entrance and pressed himself against the wall.

He picked up three distinct voices, the thumping of tankards against wood, and then the harsh rattle of dice in a cup. He peered around the entrance. Three stable hands were seated around a rotted wooden table with a small pile of coins. One was shaking a cup of dice while the other two taunted him. One pulled the cork out of a bottle of spirits and poured. Their faces were red and sweaty, and the one doing the most taunting was already barely holding his head up with his hand, his elbow precariously perched on the table's edge.

Anuhea let out a held breath and took in the rest of the stables. There were a dozen stalls on each side, and from the amount of foot stamping and stray whinnies, he assumed all of them were occupied. It took him a little bit in the dim light to notice the small window high on the back wall.

Clinging to the side of the building, Anuhea made his way to the back, pulled himself up and peeked in to make sure the stable hands were still at their game and drink and there wasn't anyone else he hadn't noticed before. Seeing that it was safe, he slipped through the window and landed with a soft sound on the dirt. He immediately slid behind the last stall and out of sight. The horse in the stall snorted and kicked at the door, rattling its hinges, and Anuhea froze, waiting for any reaction from the stable hands.

The dice clattered on the table. One of them laughed, another groaned.

Anuhea crept out and lifted the beam barring the horse's door. He eased it aside, keeping one eye on the stable hands, and opened the horse's door. The horse snorted and looked at him, and Anuhea eased back and opened the stall across. He eased back out of sight, taking the barring board with him. He waited a few seconds, and seeing that the horses weren't going to run on their own, he pitched the board up across the stalls. It crashed into a wall behind one of the trapped horses, which immediately whinnied and snorted and kicked at its door. The loud bang of the wood sent the others into a similar frenzy and sent the two free horses bolting out of the stalls.

The noise made the stable hands leap up from their game, tipping their stools and table in the process. One got tangled in the stool's legs and went down. The other two rushed out just in time to see the two horses barreling toward the exit, and they dove out of the way.

Amid their cursing and shouting, Anuhea went to the next stall and flipped off the barring bar. That horse bolted the second the door was open, and tore out of the stables. Anuhea ducked into the empty stall until he heard the stable hands' shouting diminish into the night as they chased their escaped charges. After checking that they were gone, he opened every stall and let the frenzied animals bolt out into the night. When he reached the entrance, he peered out into the courtyard filled with shouts. He saw dark shapes running through the courtyard, chasing fleeing horses.

"Remember," he'd said to Tinnu, "if you know where someone is looking, you know where you can go unseen. If you can't be sure where someone is looking, create something they can't look away from."

Anuhea took the candles from the table and went to a pile of hay. He dug out a hole and placed the candle inside, waiting for smoke to begin curling up out of it. He went to the back and lit more hay, laying the table and stools over the slowly spreading flames.

He lingered in the entrance, watching until there were faint glows of light from where he'd started his fires, and then slipped out into the darkness again.

With the chaos in the courtyard, there was much more to worry about, but Anuhea kept to the wall and hurried through the shadows. All around him were shouts and neighs and curses. Even when they rounded up all the horses, he knew that one thing was true between the old world and the new: even a small fire in a castle required everyone's attention.

The keep's doors were massive oak reinforced with iron bands, and at the top of smooth marble stairs leading to the doorway were a row of burning braziers basking the area with light. As Anuhea crouched in the last bit of shadow before them, he thought about tipping them over as well to add one more collection of flames to deal with, but he knew that he was going to be coming back out at some point, and couldn't risk an entire contingent of guards being there cleaning up when he emerged.

He scoured the area around the stairs, searching for some smaller side entrance that most would use. The main doors seemed too large to move, and he didn't know if he had the strength to make them budge, let alone open them to get in. Stretching out on either side of the doors were a number of tall windows looking out into the courtyard, but he wasn't ready to start breaking glass yet. He glanced back at the courtyard again to make sure that there were no guards rushing for him, and then darted across the light and heaved his shoulder against the door. At first it didn't move and his feet only scraped against the stone. He readjusted and shoved again, and felt the door slide just a bit. He tried a third time, and the door started to move. He stopped as soon as there was a tiny sliver wide enough for him to slip through.

The hall beyond was dimly lit from a few lanterns hanging down from the mezzanine. Anuhea froze in the doorway, watching along the banister for any movement. He hurried to one of the pillars holding up the second floor and hid in the darker shadows. His breathing seemed too loud and he took a few steadying breaths, searching for any sounds around him. Tapestries nearly covered the walls, broken only by the various corridors leading deeper into the keep.

This was the moment that had been sitting in Anuhea's chest since he had agreed to find Ivellios. Inside the citadel, each stone laid by those most loyal to Sadoc, those who desired to raise a castle to him out of the dirt and see his vision expand to every corner of this new world. The stones themselves seemed to radiate the new god's desires, and even in the darkness, even with a roof blocking the burning red star, Anuhea could feel it watching him. This was as close as he had been since the world's sundering, since watching the world break apart and Sadoc ascend into the sky on that broken piece of rock.

"Watch closely," Anuhea whispered.

He went to the nearest lantern and unhooked it from its chain. He heaved it against the nearest tapestry. Glass shattered, oil splashed, and the flame hungrily leapt free from its confines. Thick black smoke rolled off the burning oil, and the tapestry was quickly engulfed, the fire growing and licking the bottom of the balcony. Anuhea moved about the room, pulling down each lantern and pitching them against the tapestries.

As the fires spread, starting to consume wood and stretch toward the support pillars, Anuhea covered his mouth and nose with his cloak and fled, knowing that he'd already lingered too long in one place, and soon someone would be on their way to investigate the crashing.

He rushed down the right hall leading along the courtyard. Peering out the windows, he could see flickering light inside the stables and dark horses still rearing and running through the darkness. There were dozens of doors, but Anuhea was looking for a way down, and he hurried along the hall and lingered at the first junction, listening and peering for any guards. Occasionally he needed to double back and hide behind a pillar, crouch down into one of the darkest corners and hold his breath as a young acolyte wearing over sized robes rushed past with a lantern held high, the slapping of sandals echoing through the barren halls.

Slowly there were more shouts, more sounds of running. The stone walls echoed the sounds and it was easy to be tricked into thinking that the stamping boots were all around and closing in. Anuhea kept low, skulking through the halls, searching each passage, searching for stairs down, trusting his instincts to know when running feet were coming at him and when they were passing him by.

Near the back of the keep, where the building shared its wall with the wall around the entire compound, Anuhea found the stairs leading down. They were in a dark hallway, the farthest they could possibly be from the main entrance. A lantern hung on an iron hook at the top of the stairs, unlit.

Anuhea drew one of his daggers and kept it close to his body. He eased down the stairs, taking care to not scrape, not to disturb even a tiny stone that could bounce down ahead and announce his arrival. The stairs were a tight spiral and steep, and even his elvish sight struggled to make out the edges of the steps. Far below, there was a faint flicker of orange light.

The stairs ended in a small room, beyond which was a long hallway, where there was a desk with an ax sitting on it and a guard leaning back on a chair, his chin slumped into his chest. A thick ring of keys hung from his belt.

Anuhea eyed the keys. He knew he needed them, but he doubted that he would be able to get them and get Ivellios out of the cell without waking the guard. Even if the guard slept like the dead, he knew that it wasn't wise to count on him sleeping. Too many tiny things could go wrong, and he couldn't take the chance.

His fingers tightened on the hilt of his dagger. This far down, he knew there was nothing stopping him from sneaking up on the guard and slitting his throat. No chance for him to raise an alarm, and it could possibly be hours before anyone found him. One clean motion and dozens of variables dealt with. And one less Sadoc worshiper in the world.

The weight of the thought made his hands start to quiver, and then the memory of how many senseless deaths he had caused in order to expedite a job made the quiver turn into shaking so badly he couldn't even keep his fingers on the dagger's hilt.

Just thinking about taking another life was almost enough to make him imagine Tinnu's face. The way she would take what seemed like the most convoluted path through a problem, but in the end she would succeed without having to hurt anyone. In that way, she had been a better thief than he had ever been; she had been able to see so many different solutions to obstructions that he had never considered. He had been focused on getting done as quickly and cleanly as possible; she had tried to ensure that the world was a better place.

After all his instruction, she had still found a way to every goal that was exactly in her style and almost unrecognizable as a series of skills he had taught her. And now, standing behind a sleeping guard in the most secure part of a citadel devoted to his greatest enemy, he stood imagining what Tinnu might do in his place.

She would find something simple, yet elegant.

Anuhea backed up the stairs until he was well shrouded in shadow. He listened again, ensuring that there was no one coming down the stairs, and then shouted as loud as he could, "Fire! Fire! What are you still doing down here!"

The guard jerked awake and his chair's legs went out. He crashed to the ground and rolled, grabbing for his ax while Anuhea kept shouting. "We need every man in the keep! Move! Move! Fire!"

Anuhea pressed himself against the wall as the guard rushed up and past him. He lingered until he could no longer hear the guard's boots pounding stone. Then another second to make sure that such a simple trick had worked.

The hall beyond the tiny guard room was filled with rough walls and iron bars embedded straight into the stone. The floor was uneven and the ceiling was low. The only sound was the faint flicker of the flames on the torches. The cells were all empty until he came to the last one. There was a torch directly across from the cell, allowing him to look in without light falling onto his own face.

The elf chained to the wall in the cell was so battered Anuhea could not determine his age. His arms above his head, his neck secure by an iron brace in the wall. Half of the elf's face was ruined with deep fire scars, his right ear a knot of veins and hardened skin. That eye was a milky, unseeing pearl. Even unmoving, hanging limp, the iron shackles cutting into the raw, inflamed flesh of his wrists and neck, the scar tissue pulled at the corner of his mouth, so it looked like he had a humorless, perpetual smirk. His head had been shaved, and his fingers were twisted into horrible angles, the nails missing. He was naked, and his torso bore ancient, white scars interwoven with fresh cuts, ocher bruises.

The elf seemed too broken to move. But his good eye slid in its socket to stare at Anuhea's silhouette. There was fury and distrust in the eye, an old spirit that Anuhea hadn't seen since the world ended. Nothing about the elf moved, except that single eye following any subtle shift Anuhea made.

"So this is what happens to us, is it?" Anuhea said. "If they catch us?" He pushed back his hair. He stretched his jaw and said in Elvish, "Tell me your name."

The elf in the cell was silent.

Anuhea watched the way the eye moved quickly, deliberately. It was the eye of a soldier, someone accustomed to watching for and learning from the smallest of gestures. Anuhea tried to see his hands, looking for the deep callouses on his palms from years of training with a sword, but he couldn't make out such small details in the dim light.

"There can't be too many elves they have locked up around here," Anuhea said, still in Elvish. "So I'm pretty sure I'm in the right place. But I'm not about to go breaking out the wrong elf and get myself killed over nothing. I wouldn't be able to face any of them in the next life if that happened. They'd never let me hear the end of it. So tell me your name. If you're who I'm after, I'll get you out of here."

The eye was full of distrust.

Anuhea stepped up to the bars and turned his face, hoping the light would show enough of his face that the other elf could see it was one of his own. But nothing changed, and if not for the slight flicking of the elf's eye over his features, Anuhea would have feared he was already dead.

"Astra found me," Anuhea told him. Then, as a murmured afterthought in the human tongue, "No, I guess that wouldn't help you believe me, would it? They probably know all your acquaintances, don't they?"

Anuhea took a deep breath and let it out slowly. The silence in the prison was soothing, but he was on edge, listening for anything that would announce that there had been an alarm sounded he was unaware of. He looked at the elf, thinking of how he was going to get such a battered body out of the citadel, but also unwilling to even make the attempt until he was certain. Who else it might be, he couldn't imagine, but he had only come for one elf and he wasn't leaving with any others.

He thought what he could say in order to let the elf trust him. He imagined if he were in the cell who he would trust, and the list was incredibly short and all of them were dead. Unless a ghost had walked in, he would never believe a word that was told to him. Everything could be a trick to get information. He would only trust a new face if it knew something no one else could possibly know except something from the dead.

"You don't know me," Anuhea said in Elvish. "And I don't know you. But I think you've heard a story about me." He couldn't look at the elf anymore. He looked down the hall, at all the bars and uneven stones. The candle nearly melted into a pool of its own wax on the guard's table. "A story about a little girl lost in the snow. I took her in and put her next to a fire. And when she was warm and fed, I learned she had nowhere to go." He looked down at his feet. "So I kept her around. And, like a fool, I tried to teach her everything I knew."

The silence stretched out so long that Anuhea was weighing whether he took the gambit and saved the ruined elf in the cell, or if he scoured the rest of the citadel, what must have dozens of dungeons, searching for another, for they might have any number of elves they were holding, seeking to pry out the secrets of the old world, and knowing it was impossible to complete before Astra returned with the airship.

Then, a hoarse, ruined voice from inside the cell said, "My name is Ivellios Nightbreeze, captain of the queen's guard and sole surviving member of House Nightbreeze."

Anuhea looked up and stretched his neck. "Good," he said. He pulled his leather roll of tools from his belt. "Now comes the fun part."

Chapter 10: The Escape

Anuhea dropped to his knees and examined the lock. It was a bulky, iron thing, meant to withstand the worst abuse. He unrolled his tools across the floor and selected a few of the heavier picks. He placed two in his mouth while he probed the lock's interior with two more.

The tools felt like extensions of his fingers, and the familiarity of exploring a lock helped steady his hands. The metal points felt around, painting a picture in Anuhea's mind of the lock's design. In that moment, in the nearly silent prison, it almost seemed like he was back before Tinnu, before Blaz, when he was still on his own, wandering from city to city, stealing gold from anywhere that seemed to have a lot of it and using it to continue moving. He tried to seize that feeling, that feeling of lightness and freedom, but he knew that he would never have been trying to get someone out of a cell. He glanced up, and Ivellios was still unmoving with his one good eye trained on him. There was no way to think of him as a pile of gold to be smuggled back out to the street.

The lock wasn't an elaborate thing at all. Simple. Meant to keep the door on and nothing more. Anuhea smirked around the picks in his mouth. "Best locksmiths in the world were always dwarves," he said. "Look what you get when you rely on humans for everything." A few more seconds of probing, and then Anuhea depressed the pins and twisted. The lock popped open, Anuhea tossed it aside, and opened the door.

He entered the cell and looked the elf over. He knew Ivellios must have been in this prison since before Astra had found him, and the effects of that time were clear across his body. Closer, now, he could see each of Ivellios's fingers were bent at the wrong angles, the skin split and swollen. His ribs were blossomed with bruises that suggested broken ribs.

"You're not going to be able to follow me out of here, are you?" Anuhea muttered. He set to work on the shackles binding his ankles, then the iron band around his neck. Finally he reached up and undid one of the shackles on his wrist. Immediately Ivellios slumped forward, and Anuhea had to get his shoulder against his chest to keep him from collapsing and be left dangling from one wrist. Even for an elf, Ivellios's weight was light enough to make him feel hollow. Despite that, with one shoulder holding him up and his head pushed to the side, Anuhea had to fumble to blindly get his picks into the last lock and feel around for the pins. It took longer than the others, but finally the lock popped open and Ivellios's full weight fell against him.

Anuhea eased him to the ground. The elf supported himself on his own arms for a moment, and then, his entire body trembling, lowered himself fully to the floor.

"That's what I figured," Anuhea muttered around the picks still in his mouth. He pulled them out and returned them to his leather bundle, rolling it up with practiced ease and replaced it in his belt. "Let's go." He hefted Ivellios up again, getting under his arm and moving forward. Ivellios's feet slid alongside him, but most of his weight pressed down on Anuhea. To move any faster than a shuffle, Anuhea would need to drag Ivellios along.

"This isn't going to work," Anuhea said as he stooped. He slid Ivellios onto his back and lifted him. Seeing his limp hands hang down in front of him, he almost lost his balance and fell, remembering his long march with Tinnu. Even though he was larger than his sister, the weeks of confinement had made him a wisp of Tinnu's lithe weight.

So far below the ground, he couldn't hear what was happening in the citadel. There was a moment when he feared that the fires he'd started had already been extinguished and now the guards would all be scouring for whomever had started them. In a perfect heist, he would have had another way out already planned that didn't take him back through the chaos he'd left in his wake. But beyond Ivellios's cell, there was only a rough stone wall.

He pushed his wishes aside and focused on listening. He moved as fast as he could with Ivellios on his back, hurrying up the stairs while also straining for even the slightest hint of a boot scraping stone coming for him. By the time he reached the top of the stairs, his legs were already beginning to tremble and he stopped to catch his breath. He had been used to fleeing, but he had never had to carry someone on his back while he did so, and those times were all long ago. Again the memory of carrying Tinnu through the dead necromancer lands tried to stab into his thoughts, and he instinctively looked back to check if Ivellios was still breathing. All he could see was the blind pearl staring at nothing.

He crept through the halls full of doors, listening to the distant shouting and stampede of boots that occasionally welled up like thunder through the corridors. The smell of smoke was getting stronger and a haze lingered along the ceiling. He paused in shadows, lingered before turning corners, and slowly worked his way back to the windows looking out over the courtyard.

When he arrived at the first corridor off the main hall, he was greeted with light, smoke, and the roar of flames. The main hall burned bright with fire licking up the support beams; choking smog made everything hazy. Anuhea took the moment to lower Ivellios to the ground. He checked the elf, saw that his good eye still followed everything, and pressed his face against the glass. Out in the courtyard, the stables was a ball of flames and dozens of men were lined up, buckets passing between them up and down as they threw water to contain it.

Anuhea retrieved his tools again and took out his small hammer. He smashed through the glass and cleared the frames of jagged pieces. The shattering seemed deafening, and even though the roar of the flames was louder, every part of him wanted to bolt immediately at the sound. His instincts told him to retreat and hide until any investigation of the broken window was completed and then sneak out when any alert was lowered, but he knew there was no time other than this instant if he was going to make his escape.

He kicked out a piece of frame and widened his hole. After double checking that there weren't any jagged pieces of glass left, he eased Ivellios through the window feet first. He had to wrestle with the elf's shoulders to get him through the narrow opening, but Ivellios went through, and then slumped over in the grass.

Anuhea slid out after him. The courtyard was bathed in firelight, but above the sky was losing some of its blackness and approaching a deeper hue of blue. He pulled Ivellios up, got him over his shoulders like a sack of grain, and checked the line of guards at the stables. Then, from the corner of his eye, he realized another line was battling the blaze in the main hall.

A dozen of them had stopped and were looking at him. Several were pointing and shouting, their words lost in the other cacophony.

Anuhea bolted. He ran as fast as he could across the courtyard, heading for the entrance to the northern tower. All his fatigue vanished and his entire body was focused on the exertion of running, leaning forward and keeping Ivellios's weight centered. His mind was clear, focused only on the feeling of his feet against the grass, listening to all the sounds around him. He could hear guards behind him, but the roar of flames and the shouting made it impossible to tell how many. It didn't matter; escape was within his grasp and he could feel it pulling at him. He just needed to be fast enough to grab it.

In the darkness of the tower, he momentarily lost his sight but didn't slow. He took the stairs as quickly as he could, and the moment he could see their outlines again he leapt up them two at a time. The thick walls muted the flames and shouting outside, but amplified the boots thudding against stone and the shouts just behind him. He considered stopping, turning, knowing the advantage of fighting in such a narrow space, but he knew that he couldn't fight off an entire keep of guards, and he was so close.

He reached the top of the stairs and shoved open the trapdoor. The sky was deep indigo and the eastern horizon was bleeding orange. Anuhea rushed over to the eastern edge of the tower and stared off toward the horizon, breathing heavily, suddenly cool in the dawn wind.

The skies were empty all the way to the horizon.

The thud and scrape of boots made Anuhea look behind him. Guards emerged from the stairs, weapons drawn. Most were wearing simple leather vests, but one wore a hauberk and moved to the front while the others waited around the trapdoor.

The leader looked around and shook his head. "Nowhere left to run, now!" he called out. He drew a sword from its scabbard. The early light caught in the steel and made it fiery. Anuhea watched the blade, noticed that the steel was flawless, the edge without a single nick. The guard took another step forward and laughed. "This fire your doing?" He pointed with his sword. "A little distraction to get your friend out?"

"Oh, I've never met him before," Anuhea said and looked back toward the rising sun. The orange lightened, and the top of the sun came up, making him squint in the light and casting long shadows out from each crenelation and guard.

"Oh really? So you're just sneaking into citadels and nabbing random elves, are you?"

"It's the sort of thing I've been known to do, yes."

The guard snorted and motioned around the tower. "And what kind of fool escapes to the top of a tower? What? Were you going to turn into a bird and fly away?" The other guards laughed. "So are you going to come back in peacefully? We have a few questions we'd like to ask you is all. And if not," he shrugged, "we can do this the fun way."

Anuhea squinted against the rising sun. He still couldn't see anything, but his ears pricked at the distant sound of a thousand insects letting off a low hum. The wind was blowing westward, and the breeze carried the faintest scent of hyacinth.

He smiled.

"What did you say?" he called back to the guard.

"Eh?"

Anuhea lowered Ivellios to the stones and propped him against a crenelation. The elf's eye still moved, watching the guards, and Anuhea felt a lightness spreading through him. "Don't worry," he said in Elvish. "I'm going to get you out of here."

Anuhea straightened and turned to the guards. "Just before. You said something about escaping to the top of a tower. What did you say?"

The guard snorted again and looked back at his fellow guards. "Do you get this one?" he said. He looked back at Anuhea. "I thought those big ears of yours would make your hearing better. I said, 'What fool escapes to the top of a tower?'"

"Fool?" Anuhea's smile widened. "Fool? Don't you know who I am?"

The captain chuckled and looked back at his men. They all laughed with him. "Another pointy-eared traitor." He took another step forward and added, "We know just how to deal with your kind here."

"Another?" Anuhea's smile pulled up over his teeth. "Oh no. There's no one else like me. Not in this world." He threw back his head and laughed, and for the first time in a long while it was not a bitter, humorless laugh. He looked around, fully realizing that he was on top of a tower of a citadel devoted to the god who had taken everything from him. There was nowhere to go until Astra arrived, and it should have felt like a prison. But he felt something inside him cracking, crumbling apart, and dissolving into dust. Something heavy that he'd been carrying around. He glanced back at Ivellios and in sharp shadows, if he squinted just a little bit, he could make out the same curve of Tinnu's jaw, the same flare of nostril. He remembered sitting in the tavern and hearing the whispered conversations about him. He remembered the entire tavern turning the day Tinnu asked to be his apprentice. How many people had begged to travel with him and he'd turned them all away. He remembered how the world had felt so open and free, and the greater the challenge, the more energy he had to overcome it.

He looked at the guard, his sword, the oiled leather jerkins of his men. Outnumbered, nowhere to go.

Anuhea spread his hands wide, as if indicating a glamorous offering. "I'm Anuhea the Many-Handed," he said.

There was a moment silence, and then all the guards burst out laughing. "Is that so?" the leader said. He pointed with his sword. "Looks like you only have two hands there, yeah?"

Anuhea snatched a dagger from his thigh and spun it through his fingers. The motion was quick enough that some of the guards still hadn't moved to their weapons by the time he'd drawn the second. He smirked as he watched some of them struggling to get their weapon clear of their sheaths, the uncertain adjustments of their hands on the shafts of pole arms.

"You didn't hear? I once stole the beard off a dwarf and he didn't notice it was gone until the next day." He slid his feet farther apart and prepared to lunge. "I once stole everything of value from a noble while he was having dinner." He twirled his daggers. Their familiar steel felt natural against his skin, fit perfectly into his palms. His fingertips found every familiar groove in the hilts. "I once stole the moon during an eclipse, but it was too easy, so I put it back." The guards didn't chuckle. They stared at him like he was mad.

"But those are old exploits," he said. His smile faltered, and pulled into a sneer. "You would have heard of me more recently. When your god was busy breaking the world apart, I was there. I was trying to stop him."

The guard smirked. "Yeah? Sounds like you wouldn't have escaped alive, then."

"Exactly," Anuhea said. "So who do *you* think you are, trying to stop me when your god couldn't even succeed?"

He lunged forward. The guards came to meet him, but he flowed like the old days—like time was as fluid as water, like there was nothing to lose. His arms were light, his feet easily finding the grips in the porous stone. He flipped his daggers around, and when he reached the captain, he ducked under his sword arm. Anuhea jabbed the hilt of a dagger into his nose and shoved him over as he passed.

The other guards were easier—young men with little experience fighting, all regimented training. They were not used to combating someone from the old world, where there were more dangers around every corner. He flowed around their blades, struck the tops of their heads, their temples, their throats with the bottoms of his daggers. They crumpled, he flowed past. He kicked another over, and, seeing his opponents on the ground, rolling about, he pivoted and ran back to the trapdoor. More soldiers were on the stairs, and he kicked the one just emerging square in the chest and sent him falling back into the next. He turned back and ran toward Ivellios, kicking over one of the guards who was starting to regain his feet as he passed.

The hum of the forest was louder. He ran to the tower's edge and saw that the airship was near enough to blot out the rising sun. The tower dropped into shadow as the airship flew right up to it, turning at the last second. The turn lifted the side of the ship and Anuhea's vision was filled with the ship's side.

"Lower!" he screamed, hoping Astra could hear him in the depths of the ship.

A boot on stone behind him and Anuhea turned. He parried a sword with a dagger and stepped in close to his opponent. He jammed the hilt of his dagger into the guard's ribs and kicked him in the knee. He pushed the guard over and rolled around an attack from another. He jabbed his dagger's hilt into the man's back and kicked out his knee as well. When he went down, Anuhea shoved the back of his head so he went face first into the stones.

The airship began to lower, but it wobbled a bit and the side slammed into the tower. The impact shook the entire structure like an earthquake, and Anuhea dropped to his knees. He glanced to the guards and saw those who had been raising up had been knocked back down and then to Ivellios who had slumped over. The airship moved, scraping along the stones as it descended, tearing a giant, jagged gash through its wood, sending a shower of splinters into the air. The friction vibrated the entire tower, and Anuhea had a brief image of the entire thing collapsing, and then a paralyzing memory of the world shaking apart, the world filling with light, the land rising up.

He shook his head to clear the image and dashed across the trembling stones to Ivellios. The airship's deck was getting closer to level with the tower, and he knew he would only have one chance. He sheathed one dagger and shoved the other between his teeth. He grabbed Ivellios and hauled him up, dragged him to a space between two crenelations, and just as the airship's railing aligned with the tower, he shoved him as hard as he could. Ivellios hit the deck, rolled, and ceased moving with his back to him. He lay so motionless that Anuhea feared that push had been the last punishment his broken body could handle.

The airship kept descending, ripping the gouge in its side longer and deeper, and Anuhea pulled the dagger from his mouth and screamed, "Time to go!" Anuhea gripped a crenelation for balance and just about to leap down onto the ship when a hand seized his tunic and yanked him back. Anuhea hit the stones hard, rolled, and narrowly avoided the sword swung down at him. He rolled back to his feet and drew his other dagger. The guard captain stood between him and the airship, blood still gushing from his nose. The guard's eyes were wild, almost crazed with rage. Anuhea heard groans and the scrape of boots and swords against stone as the guards behind him stood. The tower was momentarily still as the airship slowed, started to right itself and turn away.

Anuhea glanced back, saw that there was no chance to get through the guards preparing for another round. He rushed forward, flowed under the guard's sword, and brought his dagger hilt up into his nose again. The guard fell back, clutching his face.

And before he realized what he was doing, Anuhea was crouched on top of the guard, his hand around the guard's neck, one dagger between his teeth and the other lifted high. He squeezed so tightly he could feel a pulse, strong and quick, beneath his fingers. His jaw throbbed from clenching his teeth.

He stared into the guard's eyes and saw the world breaking. He saw the land splitting apart, heard the roar of the world's protest. He saw all the light of god's ascension, saw a tiny, black speck as Tinnu dove into the light.

Then, the falling.

"How?" Anuhea spit around metal. The rest of the question— "How can you follow this god?"—was caught in his throat and he could only spit again, "How?" The guard's eyes bulged in their sockets. His pulse banged against Anuhea's thumb. The hand with the dagger trembled.

And Anuhea wanted to keep squeezing. He wanted to strangle the life from every soldier who swore allegiance to the god who had taken everything from him. He wanted to snuff out the life of everyone who uttered a word of praise, and bring their broken bodies to the foot of the throne of god, and throw them at his feet and say, "I've only just started. Now it's your turn."

But then he knew that he would never find her again.

His fingers slacked and the guard drew in a choking, coughing breath. He dropped the dagger in his mouth into his hand. "You're not worth losing her," he said. "How could I face her again if I broke my promise?"

He leaped off the guard and ran to the edge of the tower, sheathing his daggers as he moved. The airship was drifting away, and the distance between the deck and the tower was widening. Anuhea jumped, and the airship suddenly picked up speed and the deck pulled away just before his foot reached the edge.

He fell.

Chapter 11: The Pursuit

Rushing air filled Anuhea's ears. On one side a blur of gray stone and on the other the brown blur of wood. Then the ground rushing up. He twisted in the air, trying to get his bearings. He saw the edge of the deep gouge in the wood and reached for it, but it was too far and his fingers grabbed nothing.

Then, an arc through the air like a tree branch in a breeze, one of the ropes was just below him. He reached and the sway of the rope coming nearer him seemed too slow, like it would just miss him. His fingers brushed the coarse material, pulled it into his palm, tightened.

His arm shot out straight. His shoulder ripped out of its socket in an explosion of pain. He tried to keep his grip strong, but the strength went out of his hand and he felt the rope start to slide through. He snatched the rope with his other hand, still falling, the rope tearing through his skin and making him scream. But he slowed, stopped, his palm on fire and blood oozing out of his clenched fist and running down his arm.

Barely hanging on, Anuhea fumbled about with the spinning rope until he snagged it between his feet. Pushing himself up, he pinned the rope to his chest with his arm, the other hanging limp at his side. His shoulder spasmed and each movement sent new bolts of pain through his arm. He clung with his other arm, his hand feeling like it was on fire and blood dripping from the shredded flesh. Wind pushed against him as the airship moved, and looking down he saw the city quickly turning into the more chaotic outer limits and then suddenly green, rolling fields. He looked back and the citadel was receding.

He pushed himself up with his feet, gripped the rope to his chest, and repeated. One tiny inch at a time. Higher and higher. He squeezed his eyes shut against the pain between each movement, opening them only to ensure his footing on the rope. He pushed himself up until the deck was level with his sight. Panting, he let go of the rope and wrapped his good arm around the railing and pulled himself onto the deck.

Astra had already emerged from the bowels of the ship. She knelt at Ivellios's head, her hands hovering over him like she wanted to reach out for him but feared he had become too fragile to touch. Anuhea pushed himself away from the edge of the deck and rolled onto his back. He sucked in air, his pulse racing both from exertion and the elation that he'd done it. He'd been in and out of somewhere he wasn't ever supposed to be, with something that was never suppose to leave. He had done what many would say is impossible, and lived to tell the tale.

It had been so long since he had last felt this way. Feeling like the world was trying to stop him, but was too slow. These were the moments in the old world he had lived for, trying to find a greater challenge that would test every skill he had. When the world was still light and everything was a game. When he was young and free. The thrill brought back just a tiny taste of that world, and even though he knew beyond any doubt that world could never be reclaimed, the reminder of it was a reason to continue, a reason to keep moving and not lie down and let atrophy overcome him.

Trying to sit brought new agony to his shoulder. He held his dislocated arm in place with his burning, flayed hand and slowly stood. His legs trembled, his feet ached, and no matter how many breaths he took it seemed like his chest was empty. He leaned on the railing and looked down at the ground speeding below them. The ship was slowly ascending, making everything look smoothed out and indistinct. The speed was exhilarating, and the open air possessed a bird's sense of freedom instead of the dread of falling.

When Anuhea looked up from the ground, there were specks on the horizon. Small dots growing larger, and when Anuhea squinted, he still couldn't make out what they were, but they had to be big to be noticeable at such a distance. Even without knowing what it was, his instincts told him it couldn't be good. The feeling of weightlessness vanished and he felt heavy in the way that he had before. He stared at the specks, full of fear, realizing that there were still new tricks this new god's followers possessed.

A minute passed. Then another. Then he could make out the vague shape of ships. Five ships in the sky, and he knew that there could only be one place they'd come from.

He spun away and rushed across the deck to Astra and Ivellios, his legs quivering and his gait more of a limping lunge than a run. Astra was still kneeling beside Ivellios, her fingers glowing with the light of a sunset filtered through the leaves. Moss was sprouting along one of Ivellios's open wounds, stitching itself together and pulling the flesh closed.

"Astra," Anuhea said. She made no reaction to his voice, so he said louder, "Ships. Five from the citadel." He glanced back and saw that they were already closer. "We need to go faster."

The light blew away from Astra's fingers and she looked up.

"This is as fast as the ship can go," she said.

Anuhea looked back again, trying to formulate some plan. But he did not understand this world of airships and the magic that kept them afloat. Running through a street, there were dozens of places to hide, to lose a pursuer, so many chances to do something to make them stumble and gain distance on them. But all around them was nothing but open air. Not a cloud, not a mountain. Only sky and plains. There was nowhere to hide, no way to outmaneuver whoever the citadel had sent after him.

His bloody hand gripped a dagger hilt, an old survival instinct bubbling up beneath the agony of grooves in his wound. But even without knowing how many soldiers were packed into the airships, with his arm and hand, he'd be lucky if he'd get through the first one. Even the most skilled with a blade he'd known wouldn't have been able to fend off five ships' worth of soldiers. And even if he wasn't injured and exhausted and his entire crew was still alive and beside him, the situation would have looked dire. He looked back at Ivellios—if the stories of the queen's guard, and one skilled enough to become their captain were true, the elf might have had a chance if he could face the enemies without being overwhelmed.

But it did Anuhea little good to imagine allies he didn't have.

Astra, too, was looking across the sky to the approaching ships. "Help me move Ivellios," she said. The two of them hoisted Ivellios up and dragged him down into the depths of the ship. They took him to the cabin that had been his war room and laid him on the floor. Astra stood for a long moment, looking at him, and then abruptly turned and went into the corridor.

"We need a plan," Anuhea said, holding his arm and following her. She went deeper down into the ship.

"I have a plan," Astra said. "I'm going to kill them all."

The simplicity with which she said it made Anuhea pause. She reached the ladder and descended into the lowest part of the ship. "Wait! Astra!" Anuhea rushed to the ladder and started down, balancing on the backs of his feet to get down without using his arms while keeping Astra in his sight. "You can't kill them! That's not part of the plan."

The moss that had wilted and grayed while Astra was above deck flaked away and fresh moss sprouted along her cheek and shoulders in the light of the heart of the forest. The soothing green light shifted to cloudy, roiling clouds and the light in the room dimmed.

"You can't!"

Astra turned and looked at him. Her eyes were all animal fury and rage. "You can't," she said. She turned back to the heart of the forest and pressed her hand against the crystal. The light darkened more until the room was like night with a full moon behind clouds. Anuhea could barely make out Astra's outline. Stray sparks like lightning deep in the heart's core flashed out and threw the room into stark, harsh black and white. "What good is an oath if it means you can save no one?" she asked. "What good is an oath if it means you must watch everyone die?"

Anuhea's fingers trembled, and he knew that he wanted Astra to do it. He wanted every one of them to die for following the god who had taken everything from him. He wanted to watch their ships fall from the sky and feel the satisfaction that they had come to the same end that Tinnu had. He wanted it to happen again and again, to everyone who swore fealty to Sadoc.

But none of it would bring Tinnu back, and none of it would fill the emptiness that felt like it would consume him. All it would do would mean breaking his vow, and what good was such revenge if, in the end, he arrived in the next life unable to face her for all he had done?

"We don't make vows because they'll be easy," Anuhea said. "We make them because we believe they'll make the world a better place."

Storm clouds swirled like a hurricane was ripping through the heart of the forest. "I will make the word a better place," Astra whispered. "The world will be better with every one of them dead."

Astra's words sounded like a curse that would ripple through the rest of Anuhea's life. He knew that to uphold his promise, he would embark on a journey more difficult than any he had ever managed before. A quick, easy knife had solved so many problems, and the weight of all of them was something that he would have to carry for the rest of his life. He could imagine small pieces of it falling away as he worked and toiled to bring some of Tinnu's light back into the world. All he had left of her was that tiny speck in his memory, just before she fell so far as to vanish, and he knew that if his blades took on one more drop of blood, that drop would obliterate her.

"She wouldn't want this," Anuhea said. "She wouldn't want any of it. She would find another way. What will I tell her when I see her again?"

"Tell her that her murder is avenged," Astra said. "Tell her those who harmed her brother are defeated and he might finally find some peace." She looked into the swirling magic of the forest. "Tell her that at least some who destroyed the forest will now be food for new plants."

"Those would be the last things she'd want to hear," Anuhea said.

In the darkness, a flash of brilliant, rippling marigold. Astra's hand slid across the crystalline surface and whispered in the ancient, throaty language of her magic. Anuhea shook his head, trying to find some words that would dissuade her, some plan that would allow them to escape without destroying their pursuers. But he could only imagine the world breaking, Tinnu falling, and trying so hard to keep that tiny speck in his vision.

"We'll find a way," Anuhea said, moving forward. "Stop." He reached out with his bloody hand.

The stormy roils burned away into a brilliant, fiery light. Anuhea needed to lift his arm to shield his eyes. Squinting, peering around the edge, he saw a great bird of flames, wings spread wide, flying from deep in the heart's storm. Astra pressed her other hand against the crystal, and the entire airship shuddered. Astra continued to speak in the ancient tongue. The air filled with rippling heat like standing too near a fire. Astra uttered another sentence and then stopped. She peered into the crystal, her jaw set. The bird of flame ripped apart and tendrils of fiery light rushed out from the crystal and wrapped around Astra's arms. The light burrowed beneath her flesh, squirming deeper, but Astra's face remained unchanged. The airship shuddered again, violently enough to send a shower of dust from the ceiling. Anuhea tore his sight away from Astra and searched the ceiling then floor for any hint of a crack. The ship shook again and Anuhea clung to the ladder, suddenly fearing the ship opening up and there being nothing but endless sky below.

New moss sprouted along Astra's shoulders and down her back. Wisteria bloomed through her hair, and her hands twisted into the gnarled bark of a willow tree. She drew in a sharp breath, and when she exhaled, a cloud of pollen rippled out like smoke. The light faded, the forest returned to its usual soft green, and when Astra turned, grass sprouted about her feet in thick clumps. When she lifted her foot, the grass immediately browned, turned the raspy dry stalks of a drought.

Her eyes were full of churning flames and magic radiated from her. It filled the room, hotter than the heat from a forge. She looked at Anuhea for just a second, and then, in an instant, shrank back into the nightingale. She took flight at once and shot up the ladder and out of the room.

Anuhea didn't have time to think; he moved, almost leaping up the ladder and running through the airship after Astra, gritting his teeth against the agony in his shoulder with every step.

When he reached the deck, he couldn't find her at first. But when he looked toward the approaching airships, he saw her, the tiny speck of bird almost lost in the sky. But she was growing and the air wavered around her as it did when rising off of sun-baked stones in summer heat. Her feathers were dropping away, and suddenly there was a flash of light. Flames sprouted from her wings, rippled through the air like water over rocks, and with a shriek that was enough to make the wood beneath Anuhea's feet tremble, a phoenix emerged from Astra's diminutive form. The burning wings were stretched as wide as a dragon's and even though she was far off, Anuhea could feel the wash of heat from the transformation. A wave of hot wind buffeted the ship, rocking it so violently that Anuhea needed to drop to his knees to keep from tumbling over. Astra rose higher and higher, the flames of her body churning against themselves, stray pinions broke free from her wings and ripped apart into cinders whipped away in the swirling gale.

Anuhea watched as Astra dove, her molten body ripping through the first airship. The wood immediately burst into flames. The fires burned hot enough that it began breaking apart almost instantly. Sparks and burning boards cascaded from the rapidly deteriorating ship, and, speckled among them, larger, bright flares that flailed as they fell.

Arrows shot from the other ships, filling the sky with tiny black darts. But there was nothing they could do against a creature of fire, a creature from a world so old that even the elves hadn't been able to do anything more than revere it. There was nothing in the new world, so devoid of magic, that could be done. Astra shrieked, banked, and flew through another ship.

Seeing the plummeting soldiers, the airships being rent apart, the savage power of the old world manifested in Astra once again, Anuhea felt torn between elation and despair. Everything before him was, truly, what he had wanted to see from the top of the mountain—the destruction of everything. He had watched the world get torn apart fifty years before, and every day he wanted to watch what had been made in its place razed to the ground. He wanted every stone shattered, every tree burned, and a vast nothingness to replace everything that existed so that it matched what he had felt inside. He wanted to find a way to turn the airship around and lead Astra back to the citadel, the city, and let her strafe over every home, every garrison, every farm field until the smoke was so thick it choked out the sun and cast darkness over the entire world. Watch the black stone that had fallen from the sky and that they built the citadel upon crack and melt beneath old world fire.

The screams would be horrific, but they would begin to balance out the screaming he had heard when the world shattered. The screaming that was coming from deep inside his chest, ripping his throat raw, and the screaming that had settled into his bones so that his entire body always felt as if it was about to break apart like the world had, but there would be no one to put him back together. And he wanted their screams to be nothing to him, because they had chosen to follow, to obey, the man who had desired to be a god, the one who Anuhea had stood beside Tinnu to try and stop because they knew how many would suffer, how many would die, and yet the reality had been so much worse than what they could have imagined.

But he knew that immersing himself in so much death would not lead anywhere except to more loss. And if the callouses on his soul grew over the memories, what would he be left with?

Watching the phoenix, he could almost imagine Tinnu standing in front of it, unfazed by its heat and fury. She would not have stared it down like an opponent to be bested, but with caring compassion at its suffering.

For the first time since the world broke, Anuhea tried to remember Tinnu's voice, to hear what she would say about the burning airships, this new world, and all his hatred.

Once, she had told the bird to sleep so that others might live. She had spared everyone—even those who had wronged her—so that no one would have to see their loved ones lost. How could he wish for so much destruction with the memory of her? Tinnu, who had possessed unending forgiveness. Who had fought not for her own freedom, but for the freedom of everyone in the world. She had wanted to save everyone from death and destruction, so much that—and remembering it made Anuhea's hands seize, his chest ache, and his vision blur—just before she reached Sadoc ascending on his throne of stone, she reached for her sword. She had been ready, for the first time in her life, to take a life if it meant to save the world, and it had been that one act, that one moment where she had not been forced into a role so unlike everything else in her life, that had been the moment that she began tumbling through the endless sky.

A failure? A goal too big?

He wanted to know what she would say. What she would say knowing what she had been prepared to do, and what she would think of herself afterward. How she would have changed if she had succeeded. He could not imagine Tinnu carrying the weight of taking a life, even if it had been a life taken to save the world. It seemed too much an impossibility, and, in that way, she never had a chance to succeed.

Or had there been something he'd missed? Had that hint of steel been to slice through Sadoc? Or something nearby, some tether that would have stopped the world from breaking apart?

Watching Astra rip through the last of the airships, Anuhea also remembered that Tinnu had never let her burdens destroy her like so many others he had met. Her past haunted her, but she had never run from it. She had possessed courage that none other had, a willingness to continue moving despite what the world had done to her, continued doing to her. An elf like him in a world of humans, her life had accumulated loss like a tree gathered rings. Yet, like a tree, each loss had solidified her, had drawn her deeper into her convictions, farther from what he had taught her, using those teachings as tools to accomplish her goals.

The rage and revenge that he longed for burned hot in his soul, and threatened to flash into a conflagration that would either snuff itself out or leave nothing but ash behind.

All the airships were falling from the sky. They fell too slowly, like they were underwater. Everything had slowed, and the world was too sharp. Every image was etching into his mind, everything too flooded with light. Astra circled the falling balls of fire, shrieking out a final, triumphant call. The sound resounded from the hills, and Anuhea was certain the city could hear it, could imagine them rushing to the cathedrals and praying to their god to save them. He wanted to imagine that the screech could be heard all the way to the red star, reaching Sadoc's ears.

Would Tinnu want him to finish what she'd almost done at the breaking of the world?

Once he remembered, he could only see Tinnu's hand on the hilt of her sword, the tiny sliver of elvish metal peeking out of the scabbard the only hint that she had been about to draw the weapon. But he knew that she had not been drawing her weapon for vengeance, for revenge, even though Sadoc had already taken so much from her. It had been to save everyone else, and he knew that even if he burned every city loyal to Sadoc, even if he took his daggers and sliced the throats of every priest and every soldier, none of them would prevent what had already occurred. None of them were the ones who had taken everything from him. Only Sadoc, sitting high on his throne, was responsible. No human here had torn the world. None of them had sent Tinnu falling. And their deaths would not save anyone.

"Here, take this," he remembered her saying, handing over a blanket on a snowy day.

With the world under Sadoc's rule, how many were suffering that now needed help? How many would be pressed down into the earth with no hope for survival?

He knew that if Tinnu had survived, she would be searching for them. Those who needed help. Those who were suffering. Revenge would not save anyone; it would only create more suffering. But a helping hand in hard times would bring a little light to the world.

The airships were crashing into the ground with preternatural silence. They looked surreal, crumpling against the earth without a sound. Astra was returning, her body's flames less fluid. The fire was flickering, a trail of hot ash growing thicker behind her.

Anuhea knew with certainty that Astra and Ivellios and his paths were to never cross. Where Anuhea hoped that he could rekindle some light in the world one tiny spark at a time, the way Tinnu had, Astra would never be able to see anything less than her living enemies. Enemies living while her companions were dead. Now that Ivellios was safe, they had nothing in common. Nothing shared except their memories of Tinnu, and they did not carry her final spark in their memories, the final moment of what she stood for.

Each discarded wisp of flame shrank Astra a little more, and she started to drop more quickly from the sky. The flames sputtered, became more smoke than fire, and then there was Astra the nightingale, wobbling through the air. She fluttered wildly, shot past Anuhea's head, and hit the deck with a small thud.

Anuhea watched her, and when she didn't move, he approached. The sound of the crashing airships was finally arriving—the splintering wood, the whoosh of hungry flames. The nightingale grew, returning to Astra's elf form, but even half formed Anuhea could see the damage. Her skin smoldered, and most of her moss was only ash. Her hair was nearly gone, and the bark that had covered her hands was now flaking charcoal. When she started to inhale, she was racked by coughs that send clouds of ash from her mouth. She tried to push herself up, but her arm gave out and she hit the deck with a shower of ash. It looked like her flesh was turning to cinders, and that at any moment she might collapse into a million pieces.

Anuhea reached out for her, but she swatted his hand away. The air around her still radiated heat, and steam rose from her. She coughed another cloud of ash, managed to get to her knees, then her feet. With heavy steps, each one making more dying embers cascade from her body, her skin turning more gray, she swayed across the deck and down into the ship. Anuhea followed as close as he could, but feared that if she fell and he caught her, she would turn to cinders and pass right through his hands.

One unsteady step at a time, she went to the room where Ivellios still lay on the floor in the exact place they'd left him.

"Ivellios," Astra said from the doorway, her voice hoarse and breath ragged. "They're all dead."

Chapter 12: The Confession

The buzz of the airship was everywhere. No matter where Anuhea paced, where he tried to sit, he couldn't find a true sense of silence. On the deck, even though they'd long since flown too far to see the smoke rising from the crashed airships, it was the only direction Anuhea could look, and everything that lay in that direction filled his head with too many thoughts and too much noise to focus on what he needed to do.

He'd made a crude sling out of an old cloak to support his arm after popping his shoulder back in. His other hand he'd wrapped in an old bandage to cover the open wound. Regular movements brought stabs of pain to his shoulder and aches through his knees and feet. Everything felt swollen and ripped apart and even walking took more energy than it should. The burning itch in his hand wouldn't abate.

Finally he descended into the bottom of the ship where the heart of the forest still swirled through its greens and yellows with streaks of red, orange, and brown. He caught sight of animals darting into underbrush, birds flitting from branch to branch. He rested his head on the crystalline surface and exhaled, drew in a slow breath of forest scents. He thought the smell should remind him of home, but he had been gone so long that it only possessed the faintest twinge of nostalgia. When he'd escaped, he'd willingly left it all behind and never expected to smell it again. And now, outside of this one room in the airship, he knew that these particular scents would never exist again.

The sound of wind and distant bird calls finally calmed his mind. It allowed him to think back over everything that had happened, how far he'd come from out of the mountain and how much had been on the other side of that solitary life. His body was exhausted, his mind even more.

He looked down at his bandaged hand and watched the trembling. It was less than before, but he knew what memory slithered through there, what made him tremble so much. When he tried to close his hand, his fingers refused to obey, not because of the wounds but because of a memory lodged there. He knew the only way to stop the shaking was to pull the memory out, like pulling a thorn out of skin to keep it from getting infected.

He breathed in one more old forest smell, turned away, and made his way to the room the soldiers had used for their armory.

He'd only glanced in it before, but he'd noticed which sword had to be Ivellios's. It was the only one in its proper place, and he could easily imagine Astra returning it as one of her first actions when she'd possessed her elf's body again. As soon as he picked it up, he recognized, too, that it bore the insignia of the queen's guard on the blade just above the cross guard.

The sword was light, but Anuhea could barely grip it in his injured hand. But he made himself carry it to the war room. Without knocking, he opened the door. Astra was wrapping bandages around Ivellios's wrists and stopped when he arrived. Ivellios was dressed in old clothing and propped up against a stack of books and crates, and his table had been shoved against the wall to make space. Anuhea couldn't look at them in more than glances, but it was enough to see Ivellios's single eye trained on him with the same piercing, unflinching gaze that he had possessed while chained to the wall.

In the old world, he would have approached Ivellios in the cherry blossom grove, the sacred place where the queen's guards took their oath. He would have spoken in the forest, so that the trees could hear and remember his words, so that the birds could bear witness. But all he had was this dusty room filled with maps and books and the odds and ends of supplies a failed group of resistance fighters had cobbled together. Three elves, possibly all that remained of a race that had once spanned the entire great forest. And now, even that was gone.

Astra stepped back as Anuhea approached. He glanced at Ivellios again but saw only that his eye had followed every movement he'd made. Anuhea held out the sword toward Astra and waited. It trembled, his arm too tired to hold it outstretched and his palm in agony gripping the scabbard. He made himself look her in the eyes, and she must have understood because she took it from his hand and stepped back beside Ivellios, holding the blade sideways so that the hilt pointed to the old soldier.

Anuhea took a step back and knelt.

Even though Ivellios was not royalty, Anuhea knelt in the way one was supposed to supplicate oneself before royalty; on his knees, feet under him. He couldn't remember if he was supposed to keep his toes under and rest on the balls of his feet, or if the tops of his feet should press against the floor. It was a lesson from an old life, one that he had paid no attention to. Back then, he thought that he would never bow before anyone, especially the nobility. Furthermore, he would never have to apologize for anything he'd done. Never need to seek forgiveness, especially in the formal fashion. He always thought aristocrats would want him to be in the most uncomfortable position, and he rearranged his feet. Both ways were uncomfortable, but not excruciating. He pressed the tops of his feet against the floor, so that he could not spring forward; could not easily retreat.

He did remember, though, to only look at Ivellios's feet. To never lift his eyes to see what reactions his words caused. To not see if his hand clenched in rage or softened in forgiveness.

"You might have heard of me," Anuhea said in Elvish, using the most polite endings to his words, knowing that his time away had slurred his enunciation, pushed his pronunciation closer to the human tongue. He stumbled on a few phrases, forgetting their emphasis, forgetting their tonality, but he didn't stop. "I am Anuhea the thief, sentenced to be exiled for crimes against the crown, the one who escaped from the sky prisons before punishment could be rendered."

For a fraction of a second, Anuhea had the full realization that he had rescued the last member of the queen's guard. He wondered if old grudges and old loyalties could survive the end of the world. If Astra had heard of him, would the queen's guard still have a price on his head? Would his betrayal of the crown supersede the saving of a life?

He fought the urge to look up and continued, staring down at the wooden floor. His mouth was as dry as cold ashes. "But these crimes are not the ones I come to confess to you. I want to tell you about your sister." He swallowed, but the motion was like trying to force a stone down his throat. "Once, I found a girl lost in the snow. She was cold and hungry and at first, I tried to turn her away. But I had surrounded myself with companions far more compassionate than I. When they chastised me for my callousness, I took her in and placed her next to the fire. When she was warm and fed, I learned that she had nowhere to go. So I took her as my student. I tried to teach her everything I knew. How to run. How to hide. How to fight.

"But I forgot to teach her how to have a stony heart. How to value herself above all others. These were lessons I should have taught her, but they were lessons she never would have mastered."

Anuhea's fingers hooked, shaking and unable to straighten. He wanted to hide them, but his shoulder burned and he forced his other hand to stay where it was, fingers digging into his knee. "When the world started to end, your sister took everything I'd taught her and followed the man who sought to become a god. And I, foolishly, believed in my student so much that I thought she would succeed. That she could stop him from achieving his goal and save the world from suffering."

The calloused feet, the dusty grooves in the floor blurred into watery bands of light. "We were there, at the ending of the world. The earth splitting apart. Continents rising into the sky, the sky suddenly thrust between land. I saw that we had lost. That everything we had done had failed. And I tried to tell your sister that it was time to run. Time to flee." His papery tongue licked his parched lips. "The one lesson she never learned."

He was silent for a few minutes. "There was so much light. But there it was, cutting through all that light. A path. A few stray pieces of land rising up, right to where Sadoc stood, wrapped in primordial magic, ascending into the sky. I saw it, but still started to retreat. Your sister saw it too, but she advanced.

"She almost made it. Darting up with all the speed, all the balance, all the quickness we'd practiced over the years and she'd honed on her own. One more half step and she would have had him. Could have prevented all of this. But there was something there. Some defensive magic. Just a small push." He tried to continue, but the words wouldn't come out. His tongue refused to move. He tried again. And again.

Finally, he said, "She fell. She fell into that never ending sky that we now float in. She fell from the remains of the world and vanished into nothingness."

Anuhea tried to open his fingers, but they were rigid and shaking. He tried to close them, but his fingers could only remember trying to catch her, and could not close with the fear that that they would again close on empty air.

"If I had turned her away on that snowy night, she might have had a chance. If I had refused to teach her, she might have had a chance. If I had refused to follow her when she came to me and asked for my help stopping Sadoc, she might have had a chance. But I did none of those things.

"Because of me, Tinnu is dead."

He waited for the sound of elvish steel against scabbard. He waited for the phantasmal whisper as the steel softly sliced air. The anticipation made all his muscles tense, but he exhaled slowly, willed himself to go against all of his instincts to dart, to flee, to hide again. He willed his muscles to relax and wait for what was to come. His fingers uncurled, and lay flat on his knee, hung limp from his sling. The sound of blood pounded in his ears, and beyond that the buzzing of the airship. Slowly his vision cleared and he saw the wet spots speckling the floor.

He was suddenly so tired. His entire body ached, and all the strength left him. He could easily imagine the sword rising up, poised for a moment, and then coming down. Ivellios was probably the greatest swordsman left alive in the world; he knew the elf would strike quick and true. After all this time, he could finally rest and see all his old friends again.

"Anuhea," Ivellios said, his voice still raspy and rough. Each syllable rumbled in his throat. "I dreamed one day I would speak with you."

Though there was an edge to his voice, a hardness that befitted an old soldier, there was also a compassion so out of place that Anuhea looked up. The elf's scarred face was permanently twisted, but the other half of his face rested with a small, gentle smile. He was looking straight at Anuhea.

"Did Tinnu tell you," he said, "about how I sent her away? Trying to save her, I doomed her to the difficult life that she lived. I was supposed to come and find her, but I, too, possess my failures." He didn't look away when he said it. "I have so many fond memories of her as a child, but beyond that, our paths barely crossed. Our time together was so limited. But when I saw her again, after so many years apart, I was amazed at who she'd become. How strong she was. How confident, even as she struggled."

He drew in a deep breath and let it out slowly. "All I really know of her life is that she was your apprentice. When she came to the forest, this was what she mentioned. These were the stories she told me." He glanced at Astra and she set his sword aside on the table. Once the blade was down, she returned to wrapping bandages around Ivellio's wounds. Ivellios looked at Anuhea and said, "In truth, I am certain you knew my sister better than I. Please, tell me about her."

Anuhea's body quivered and Ivellios's face blurred. "She was relentless," Anuhea said. "When she wanted to know something, she never stopped. When she couldn't succeed, she would try again. And again. She was always the last one awake, trying to solve whatever puzzle had been placed in front of her."

"She sounds like the perfect apprentice."

Anuhea nodded. "In many ways."

Ivellios nodded. "What else?"

Anuhea talked. He talked about watching her learn how to pick every lock in his collection. How she picked the lock on the chest he kept the locks in so that she could practice when he was asleep. He talked about running through the woods, learning to plan a path through obstacles without slowing. He talked about teaching her how to keep her face from showing any fear, to keep her advantage over the enemy. How every danger she found herself in was because she saw someone needing help and wouldn't stop until whatever the problem was had been solved.

The words flowed out of him like blood from a cut; like rain from the sky after a deadening drought.

Chapter 13: The Debt Paid

The airship settled down in a small clearing in a forest, and the hum of magic keeping it in the air faded. At first there was silence, but then there was the whisper of wind through millions of leaves. Birdsong. Anuhea watched the branches bend with the wind, watched all the leaves brush against each other. The forest was thin, ages younger than the elf forest had been when he'd left it behind, but the smells and the sounds still brought back a feeling of something like being home.

They had left the second layer behind, flown to the third where forests still covered the land. None had followed after Astra destroyed the airships, and she and Ivellios had taken the time between to rest. Ivellios grew stronger with each day, while Astra seemed to be weakening. The bark on her skin had settled into pallid gray, and her moss didn't regrow. She bore deep, black streaks across her body as if she had tattooed ash beneath her skin. Each day, she spent longer and longer as a nightingale, and even then her feathers were ashen and her feet blackened.

Anuhea hadn't asked where they were going, hadn't been concerned with anything except that they were not being followed. He had looked down into the deep expanse of endless sky, and all he could do was think that he had succeeded in what could only feel like his final task. He had saved the one part of Tinnu left in the world, and now he didn't know what to do. He realized that he had been expecting to die the entire time, and now that he was still alive, the world was opening up all around him. He felt like he could go anywhere until night fell and the red star came out in the sky, watching. He knew that nowhere would be safe in this new world, but he was still in it.

Listening to the trees, the birds, it felt like he had stepped back in time. He was once again in a deep forest where he wouldn't remain. It felt like a new beginning, but different this time. His actions in the citadel meant that he would always have to run, and he knew that even if he went back into hiding, Sadoc wouldn't allow him to rest ever again. Instead of a world of freedom awaiting him, it was a world of skulking through shadows and secrecy.

Such an amazing challenge.

"You have been standing here a long time," Ivellios said behind him.

Anuhea turned and the elf, though still moving slowly, carried a

"""

bulging travel bag and wore his sword again. He moved with shuffling steps and approached to stand beside Anuhea at the deck's edge. He looked at him for a minute and then looked off into the trees as well. His fingers were straight again from Astra's painstaking care to right them and breathe some healing magic into them. He bore fresh scars and bandages were still wrapped around his wrists.

"You have the look of someone lost."

Anuhea smirked. "I suppose you could say that." He glanced at Ivellios, at the queen's guard sword at his side. Even with so much time passed, he didn't feel comfortable standing next to a member of the group who had caught and imprisoned him. "Honestly, I didn't expect to make it out of there alive," he said. "Or I think somewhere deep down, I expected you to kill me when you heard what happened." A bird dropped from a tree and vanished in a flash of red into the underbrush. "And yet here I am. One more ghost from the old world wandering around the new."

"A second chance at life is not something many experience," Ivellios said. "Even in a world such as this, a life is not something to be wasted." They were both silent for a moment, and then Ivellios said, "It can be hard to learn how to walk again when you suddenly put down a heavy weight." He touched the ruined side of his face. "Just like it can be hard to see when you lose something."

Anuhea looked up at the sky, but the sun was too bright to see Sadoc's burning star. "All I ever wanted was to be free," he muttered. "And look at this mess."

"Perhaps you can be again," Ivellios said. He straightened and faced Anuhea fully and waited until Anuhea turned to look at him. "Anuhea the Exile," he said in the most formal tone and intonation of ceremony, "as captain of the queen's guard and last surviving member of a royal household, I hereby absolve you of all crimes you might have committed in the past. Your exile is revoked, and you may once again travel freely in any land belonging to the elves."

With a small smile, Anuhea said, "I don't think the kingdom of the elves are the ones I have to worry about these days."

"Going forward, I suspect that you will need the luxury of not worrying about old grudges." He started away, but stopped just at the edge of Anuhea's sight.

"My thanks to you, Anuhea. It brings me peace to know that, if my sister had to die, she died trying to defend the defenseless. I do not think I could have helped shape her into a better person, could have guided her to be the person she became. The world was certainly a better place while she was in it, and I hope that her spirit can continue even if she is gone." He walked off without another word.

Anuhea kept watching the wind pushing the trees. Astra as a nightingale landed on the railing not far away.

"We are going," she said.

Anuhea nodded. "To find another army? To wage another war?"

The nightingale looked away. "Our one chance to succeed has passed. The cities of Sadoc have spread too far and their armies are too numerous. There is nothing left we can do, just the two of us. We have been defeated, and now we shall go deep into the forest. Hopefully we will be able to find a place where we can live peacefully, as we might have in the elf lands, before Sadoc's armies find us again. Our days of fighting are over."

The bird trained her depthless, beady eye on Anuhea again. "I also owe you my thanks, Anuhea. It seems I was right to seek you out. I hope that you feel your debt to the dead is finally paid."

One of her feathers dropped off and, as it fell, dissolved into ash that floated away on the wind. Anuhea watched until the last specks vanished. "And you, Astra? What about your debt to the dead?"

"Some will rest more soundly, now, I am certain. But I fear that they are beyond my help. And, in truth, it was never my role to avenge them. Perhaps Ivellios would have served that role well, but neither of us truly know how to care for the dead, it seems. We will have to discover that, in time."

She looked down at Anuhea's steady hands. "You look lighter than when I first met you."

Anuhea flexed his fingers. "If I slow down too much, Sadoc will certainly get me." He looked up to where the red star would be burning at night. "I don't think he'll let me get away with this. Or all the other trouble I'm going to cause him."

"You will continue to fight?"

"Fight? In my way. I still have my promise. But I'm not going to let Sadoc take over everything and just sit and watch him do it. I already did that too long, so I'm going to need to make up for lost time."

"I know that you do not have use for the weapons and armor, as you said you're not a soldier," Astra said, "but the airship is yours. If you truly plan to fight against Sadoc, take it and fly. Fly faster than any of them so they cannot catch you."

Anuhea cocked his head to the side. "I figured you would need it to keep running from Sadoc."

"Ivellios and I are done fighting. This ship has served us well, but it will not be of use to us where we are going." She looked down into the forest and her voice grew small. "And I did not honor my vows. What I swore to the forest when I became a Wild One and what I have done since the forest was destroyed are not congruent. The magic I borrowed from the forest's heart are not powers I was ever meant to have. My bond with the forest was already tenuous, after what I'd done, and to summon them was enough to shatter whatever remained. The forest has taken pity on me, and gifted me enough magic to keep going, but who knows for how long. I am a Wild One without a forest, without a homeland. I will most likely crumble to dust quite soon, but perhaps we can find a place to reaffirm my vows and begin again what I was meant to do: protect the natural world. I've severed my ties for my revenge, and I have no regrets. But vengeance is not a way to live. One cannot survive that way. The forest knows this, and I did, once. I need to remember it."

She looked toward the bottom of the ship. "This ship is not payment for a deed done well. It is another burden that I ask of you. Take care of the forest for me," she said. "It deserves a proper guardian. A better one than I was."

Anuhea nodded. He wasn't sure what to say, but he opened his mouth to give some parting words. Before he could utter one, Astra alighted from the railing and darted away with quick wing flutters. She flew across the deck of the airship and vanished down over the edge. Anuhea followed her, and when he reached the other end, he arrived just in time to see her diminutive form land on Ivellios's shoulder. Anuhea watched them walk off into the woods, waiting until even the faintest of their footsteps vanished and the songs of birds returned as if no one had passed by to disturb them.

He looked up at the expansive sky, clear of any clouds. He still felt exhausted and tired, but there was a twinge of old energy starting to form in his gut. What he would do with it, he couldn't yet formulate, but he never imagined that he would be standing on a ship that could take him into the skies and be at the mercy of nothing except his own desire of where to go. The perfect freedom.

He went down into the ship and looked into each room, at the old equipment and supplies that belonged to ghosts. He went through the ship, running his hands along the walls, familiarizing himself with the feel of the wood, the warmth of it. The inside was silent when not in flight, and the only sound was his own boots scraping the floor. He stopped and listened.

The image of Anuhea's old friends came to him again, and he imagined that it must be where they were, in the next life, waiting for him. In a warm tavern, next to the fire. Cups always full of ale. Maybe even their old barkeep was there with them, the one that let them stay on credit before they were famous. That young bard strumming a lyre in the corner. The place they always went back to. He couldn't imagine a better place, but it was also where stories abounded. His friends had all been dead long enough that they would have told all their old stories many times over already. They needed some new tales to hear, and he knew that they were waiting for him to come and tell them something grand. Starting with stealing Tinnu's brother from the grips of the new god would be a good start, but it certainly wouldn't keep them entertained for eternity.

He went down into the bottom of the hull, where the soft green illumination of the forest's heart shifted across the walls. Anuhea sat down in front of it and watched the light, listened to the wind and the birds. He caught glimpses of the old world deep inside it. He rested and let the memories of everything he lost wash over him. But he had to put them down, as painful as it was. He closed his eyes and the sounds of the forest wrapped around him and it was easy to imagine being back in the forest, in a grove with the sun on his face.

He waited, hoping that he would hear Tinnu's footsteps come up behind him. A tiny snap of twig or a scrape against stone.

"Are you there?" he asked.

"Hey, Tinnu. Your brother's safe. I did it." He strained his ears, searching for any hint of phantasmal sound. When there were only the forest sounds, he gave a small smile. "Hey, Tinnu. I have some stuff to take care of yet. So wait around for me, yeah? But don't worry—I won't forget my promise."

An image came to him then, of all the street urchins that Tinnu had taken food and blankets to. They were all standing in front of him, in their rundown slum, looking up at him expectantly the way they had when Tinnu came in calling that there was fresh, warm bread. The distant sounds of the city and a bitter winter wind howled so realistically it felt like he was back there. They were all looking at him, and he tried to tell them that he didn't have anything for them, not like Tinnu had. But the first one reached out his hand and plucked a small portion of Anuhea's worry. The child closed his hand and rushed off into the alley, vanishing.

One by one, they pilfered each of his worries, each of his regrets, every fragment of his pain, and soon he was willingly handing them off to the ones that would surely know exactly where Tinnu was hiding, the ones who she had cared for when the rest of the world had abandoned them.

When the last child ran off, Anuhea opened his eyes. The room was still small, the light of the forest contained within the crystal. He felt like he was full of wounds that would slowly harden into scars. But there would be time for that.

He stood up and flexed his fingers. "So," he said to the heart of the forest, "what do you say? I made a promise to you, too. Let's go make go make a god really mad."

Acknowledgements

My deepest thanks to Janet, Crescenda, and especially Bleu for helping me meet these characters and explore their world.

Elsewhen Press

delivering outstanding new talents in speculative fiction

Visit the Elsewhen Press website at elsewhen.press for the latest information on
all of our titles, authors and events; to read our blog; find out where to buy our
books and ebooks; or to place an order.

Sign up for the Elsewhen Press InFlight Newsletter at
elsewhen.press/newsletter

The Vanished Mage

Penelope Hill and J. A. Mortimore

A vanished mage…

A missing diamond…

The game is afoot.

"From Broderick, Prince of Asconar, Earl of Carlshore and Thorn, Duke of Wicksborough, Baron of Highbury and Warden of Dershanmoor, to My Lady Parisan, King's Investigator, greetings. It has been brought to my attention that a certain Reinwald, Master Historian, noted Archmagus and tutor to our court in this city of Nemithia, has this day failed to report to the duties awaiting him. I do ask you, as my father's most loyal servant, to seek the cause of this laxity and bring word of the mage to me, so that my concerns as to his safety be allayed."

The herald delivered the message word-perfect to The Lady Parisan, Baroness of Orandy, Knight of the Diamond Circle and Sworn Paladin to Our Lady of the Sighs. Parisan's companion, Foorourow Miar Raar Ramoura, Prince of Ilsfacar, (Foo to his friends) thought it a rather mundane assignment, but nevertheless together they ventured to the Archmagus' imposing home to seek him. It turned out to be the start of an adventure to solve a mystery wrapped in an enigma bound by a conundrum and secured by a puzzle. All because of a missing diamond with a solar system at its core.

Authors Penelope Hill and J. A. Mortimore have effortlessly melded a Holmesian investigative duo, a richly detailed city where they encounter both nobility and seedier denizens, swashbuckling action, and magic that is palpable and, at times, awesome.

ISBN: 9781915304186 (epub, kindle) / 9781915304087 (212pp paperback)

Visit bit.ly/TheVanishedMage

The Harlequin: The Draper's Reel

J. A. Mortimore and Penelope Hill

Question my honesty if you must, but nobody, and I mean nobody, questions my skill.

I've never paid much attention to the gods, which may be why I foolishly agreed to steal Pardeem's reel. It seemed a straightforward enough challenge for a master trickster like me, but with things like this you never know.

Leaving my cosy retirement isn't difficult. Wearing the Harlequin's hat again feels right. However returning to Emor holds challenges. Old friends and enemies wait in the shadows; maybe I can turn that to my advantage. But now my own god seems to be paying me far too much attention. This isn't going to be straightforward.

But that's the thrill, isn't it? To dance with peril, to spin with the twists, to confound expectations and to embrace the trick for its own sake. The Harlequin doesn't give up at the first hurdle.

If I can carry this off, it will be the heist of a lifetime. Failure might cost me everything.

ISBN: 9781915304551 (epub, kindle) / 9781915304452 (226pp paperback)

Visit bit.ly/HarlequinDrapersReel

You might also like

THE WITCH'S JOURNEY

KEITH MILLER

A key may unlock more than just a door.

In a town beset by demons, from which the children are disappearing, redheaded Mira grows up wild and willful. When she's around, soups boil over and flowers catch fire, and one night in her sleep she unwittingly turns her house around.

The morning of her thirteenth birthday, Mira receives a gift from the river: a gold key. It will lead her on a journey, to seek the door her key will open.

The Witch's Journey is a dark fairytale embroidered with fairytales, full of sorrows and terrors, heartbreaks and delights, chocolates and mayhem and magic.

"A book to savor as you would fine chocolate: rich, dark, dreamlike, familiar as a fairytale, sweet as sin. I adored it."

– **Alix E. Harrow**, Hugo Award–winning
author of *The Once and Future Witches*

"Such a special story; the kind that steps into your dreams then wakes you with the taste of chocolate on your lips as a shadow in the corner walks away, and you are left remembering a place you've read about and a witch you suspect knows you've been there, and it all feels like the most delicious secret. I loved this book!"

– **Mary Rickert**, World Fantasy Award–winning
author of *The Memory Garden*

"This is rich and delicious magic for the bravest of readers."
– **William Alexander**, US National Book Award–winning
author of *Goblin Secrets*

ISBN: 9781915304933 (epub, kindle) / 9781915304834 (226pp paperback)

Visit bit.ly/TheWitchsJourney

The Sundering Chronicles by Mark Iles
I: Gardens of Earth

Imagine an alien life force that knows your deepest fear, and can use that against you.

Corporate greed supported by incompetent surveyors leads to the colonisation of a distant world, ominously dubbed 'Halloween', that turns out not to be uninhabited after all. The aliens, soon called Spooks by military units deployed to protect the colonists, can adopt the physical form of an opponent's deepest fear and then use it to kill them. The colony is massacred and as retaliation the orbiting human navy nuke the planet. In revenge, the Spooks invade Earth.

In a last-minute attempt to avert the war, Seethan Bodell, a marine combat pilot sent home from the front with PTSD, is given a top-secret research spacecraft, and a mission to travel into the past along with his co-pilot and secret lover Rose, to prevent the original landing on Halloween and stop the war from ever happening. But the mission goes wrong, causing a tragedy later known as The Sundering, decimating the world and tearing reality, while Seethan's ship is flung into the future. The Spooks win the war and claim ownership of Earth. He wakes, alone, in his ejector seat with no sign of either Rose or his vessel. When he realises that his technology no longer works, his desperation to find Rose becomes all the more urgent – her android body won't survive long in this new Earth.

ISBN: 9781911409953 (epub, kindle) / 9781911409854 (264pp paperback)

Visit bit.ly/GardensOfEarth

II: A Voice in the Darkness

A gateway and a changeling on a colony world, prompt a return to Earth to confront the aliens.

When children on the colony of Semillion go missing they return changed, the parents even claim they are not their offspring. Sherrif Andrews soon finds himself investigating the bizarre situation. What he discovers leads to him being recalled by the military and sent back to Earth, a place now quarantined and where colonial humans are forbidden to venture. The intention is to recruit ex-commando Seethan Bodell, who's living with the survivors of The Sundering and the mythological creatures that now inhabit the world.

Earth is still ruled with an iron fist by the alien Spooks, but there is something else going on behind the scenes, a new and deadly threat. To succeed, Andrews and Bodell need to call on that grand tapestry of inhabitants: the shapeshifters, elves, the ravening pack of werewolves that Seethan now belongs to, and even the dead; in the hope that it will be enough to prevent an escalating situation that could so easily lead to war.

ISBN: 9781915304575 (epub, kindle) / 9781915304476 (192pp paperback)

Visit bit.ly/AVoiceInTheDarkness

You might also like

The Avatars of Ruin series by Tej Turner
Book 1: Bloodsworn

"Classic epic fantasy. I enjoyed it enormously" — **Anna Smith Spark**

"a stunning introduction to a new fantasy world" — **Christopher G Nuttall**

"This is epic fantasy with a touch of the mythic to it. There were villains I loved to hate, and a queer protagonist I loved rooting for. Action, magic, a world in peril…what more could you ask for?" — **Trip Galey**

It has been twelve years since the war between the nations of Sharma and Gavendara. The villagers of Jalard live a bucolic existence, nestled within the hills of western Sharma, far from the warzone. They have little contact with the outside world, apart from once a year when Academy representatives choose two of them to be taken away to the institute in the capital. To be Chosen is considered a great honour… of which most of Jalard's children dream. But this year, their announcement is so shocking it causes friction between villagers, and some begin to suspect that all is not what it seems. Where are they taking the Chosen, and why? Some intend to find out, but what they discover will change their lives forever and set them on a long and bloody path to seek vengeance…

ISBN: 9781911409779 (epub, kindle) / 9781911409670 (432pp paperback)
Visit bit.ly/Bloodsworn

Book 2: Blood Legacy

"a nuanced, smart high fantasy novel with intelligent, complex characters, good LGBT rep and some killer twists" — **Joanne Hall**

"an exciting book which ups the stakes, mixing traditional fantasy with an element of possession horror" — **David Craig**

"a journey into Fantasy, only it's not quite the journey you expected, and it's all the better for it" — **Allen Stroud**

The ragtag group from Jalard have finally reached Shemet, Sharma's capital city. Scarred and bereft, they bring a grim tale of what happened to their village, and a warning about the threat to all humanity. Some expect sanctuary within the Synod to mean an end to their hardships, but their hopes are soon dashed. Sharma's ruling class are caught within their own inner turmoil. Jaedin senses moles within their ranks, but his call to crisis falls mostly on deaf ears, and some seek to thwart him when he tries to hunt the infiltrators down.

Meanwhile, Gavendara is mustering its forces. With ritualistically augmented soldiers, their mutant army is like nothing the world has ever seen.

The Zakaras are coming. And Sharma's only hope of stopping them is if it can unite its people in time.

ISBN: 9781911409991 (epub, kindle) / 9781911409892 (474pp paperback)
Visit bit.ly/Blood-Legacy

The Avatars of Ruin series by Tej Turner

Book 3: Blood War

"Smoothly throttles up a gear from the previous two books. The diverse and fleshed out characters face the desperate horrors of war, leading to a thrilling climax. An excellent addition to a gripping series." – **David Craig**

Sharma stands on the precipice of destruction as Gavendara's army of shapeshifters surges towards the Valantian mountains. A mutant invasion leaving terror and death in its wake and whose victims rise again, swelling its ranks.

Yet still the Synod dithers, its leaders fractured as they plot and scheme against each other. Jaedin is now a fugitive, Bryna's powers are waning, and Rivan grapples with the consequences of his resurrection – as well as the ominous entity that now lives beneath his skin. Whilst Miles, torn between loyalties, faces an impossible choice that could reshape the fate of nations.

Meanwhile, to the east, Elita seeks sanctuary within the enigmatic depths of Babua's jungle. The people who dwell there are distrustful of her, but for a good reason. She indeed has secrets, and it seems that trouble has followed her.

ISBN: 9781915304360 (epub, kindle) / 9781915304261 (450pp paperback)
Visit bit.ly/Blood-War

Book 4: Blood Ruin

Coming soon

Tej Turner is an SFF author and travel-blogger. His debut novel *The Janus Cycle* was published by Elsewhen Press in 2015 and its sequel *Dinnusos Rises* was released in 2017. Both are hard to classify within typical genres but were contemporary and semi-biographical with elements of surrealism. He has since branched off into writing epic fantasy and has an ongoing series called the *Avatars of Ruin*. The first instalment – *Bloodsworn* – was released in 2021, and its sequel *Blood Legacy* in 2022. The third – *Blood War* –was published in early 2024.

He does not have any particular place he would say he is 'from', as his family moved between various parts of England during his childhood. He eventually settled in Wales, where he studied Creative Writing and Film at Trinity College in Carmarthen, followed by a master's degree at The University of Wales Lampeter.

Since then, Tej has mostly resided in Cardiff, where he works as a chef by day and writes by moonlight. His childhood on the move seems to have rubbed off on him because when he is not in Cardiff, it is usually because he has strapped on a backpack and flown off to another part of the world to go on an adventure.

He has so far clocked two years in Asia and two years in South America, and when he travels, he takes a particular interest in historic sites, jungles, wildlife, native cultures, and mountains. He also spent some time volunteering at the Merazonia Wildlife Rehabilitation Centre in Ecuador.

Firsthand accounts of Tej's adventures abroad can be found on his travel blog at https://tejturner.com/

About Michael Kellichner

Michael Kellichner is a poet and writer who grew up in central Pennsylvania, but the call to see the world proved too much to stay put. Now, he's settled in South Korea with his wife and daughter and spends his days teaching ESL to children and trying to find consistent time to write. He dabbles in poetry when not working on speculative fiction, and some has even made it out into the wild. Michael's short stories can be found in various magazines, many for free online, such as *Kaleidotrope*, *The Colored Lens*, *Marrow Magazine*, and *Toronto Journal*, with more hopefully to come.

www.ingramcontent.com/pod-product-compliance
Lightning Source LLC
Chambersburg PA
CBHW051703180726
48283CB00004B/1196